PURPLE INK PRESENTS

SAVAGE SISTERS

CHANEL

iUniverse LLC
Bloomington

PURPLE INK PRESENTS SAVAGE SISTERS

This is a work of fiction. All of the characters, names, incidents, organizations, and dialogue in this novel are either the products of the author's imagination or are used fictitiously.

iUniverse books may be ordered through booksellers or by contacting:

iUniverse LLC
1663 Liberty Drive
Bloomington, IN 47403
www.iuniverse.com
1-800-Authors (1-800-288-4677)

Because of the dynamic nature of the Internet, any web addresses or links contained in this book may have changed since publication and may no longer be valid. The views expressed in this work are solely those of the author and do not necessarily reflect the views of the publisher, and the publisher hereby disclaims any responsibility for them.

Any people depicted in stock imagery provided by Thinkstock are models, and such images are being used for illustrative purposes only. Certain stock imagery © Thinkstock.

ISBN: 978-1-4917-2114-8 (sc)
ISBN: 978-1-4917-2115-5 (e)

Library of Congress Control Number: 2014900771

Printed in the United States of America.

iUniverse rev. date: 01/29/2014

I dedicate this book

To

The late Great Clarissa "Peaches" Savage

And

John Lee "Cornbread" Savage

Gone but not forgotten

I miss you both

Love

Chanel

Acknowledgements

First and foremost ALL PRAISES TO ALLAH for giving me the talent, creativity, and patience to attain my goals.

Mommy aka Momma Cakes I would not be here if it were not for you. Thank you for your support, and words of wisdom over the years. I love you.

My Husband Gene, you are my rock. I asked for love and you gave it to me unconditionally. I love you more and more every day.

My children Goo, Hass, Moody, and Middy you guys are my heart. I keep going every day because of you. I love you so much.

My sisters Sabrina Stephens and Tynisha Mitchell I love you both very much. Keep striving you can be anything in this world.

Uncle James thanks for always being there for me. You have always supported me, and taught me even when I didn't want to listen. I love you.

Uncle Kevin you don't even know, but you having me free styling in the basement, on the turn tables started something. I can't rap, but

I can put together a story on paper. I love you for always being that funny uncle who had my back.

My two closest cousins Kevina and Charice more like sisters, we grew up together, and although we don't talk every day I love you both.

Lil Calvin you are like my little brother you are such an inspiration to me. You are a fighter. I love how you strive so hard to be all you can be. Keep Striving. I love you. I will always be here for you.

Aunt Ernestine and Aunt Rose Lee thanks for your support throughout my childhood, and always being that home to come too when I had nowhere to go. I Love you both.

Aunt Alicia Thanks for always being there for me growing up. Your house was always like a second home, and you never turn anyone away. I love you so much.

Aunt Evette and Grandma Jean thanks for always being there for me, and supporting me. I may not keep in touch, but I do love you both very much.

Ms. Janice Sutton thank you for being my first critic. You read my manuscript, and encouraged me to continue to write. Thank you so much.

Ms. Rochelle Certain thanks for being that morning gossip in the morning that always got my creative juices flowing. I am waiting on our collaboration.

Aiesha Chambers a great friend and motivator. Your talks kept me motivated. You encouraged me to be an entrepreneur, and get my hustle on. You were more than a friend like a big sis. Luv ya girl.

Ms. Conklin who gave me my first Novel 100 dresses, and Ms. Amy Lynn Williams who introduced me to Ramona Quimby and Bunniculla Book Series. You guys were two of my best teachers part of the foundation that made me into the women I am today.

R.I.P lil cuzin Sade I am so sad I lost you this year. I am going to truly miss you. Especially you telling me off. You were a special person, and will always have a place in my heart.

To my lil cuzin Kareem keep your head up, I miss you, and love you. Tasha Savage another special cousin thanks for always being there to support us. Love you for that girl.

To authors like Omar Tyree, Terri Woods, and Sister Soldier thanks for paving the way for authors like me.

Anyone I might have forgot thanks for any support that you gave me. I appreciate any, and everything anyone does to for me.

Love Always

CHANEL

Chapter 1

Big Sterling

Sterling sold three kilos of coke to one of his loyal customers. As he walked from the back office of his number house, he noticed two guys playing pool, who looked like they were up to no good.

"I know these motherfuckers ain't trying to rob me," he said, giving them a death stare.

He answered his phone after it vibrated in his pocket.

"Starks, are you on your way?" asked his wife, Ms. Sandy, before he had a chance to say hello.

"I will be home soon. I am trying to get these little niggas out of here. They don't look right to me," Big Sterling said.

"I am waiting for you. Be safe, Starks, and don't do anything crazy," Ms. Sandy said.

"All right," he said, hanging up.

"Hey young'uns, I'm closing," Sterling said with attitude.

"All right, we're finishing up this game, old head," one of them said.

The two guys were dressed in black hoodies that barely revealed their faces. Sterling nodded as he wiped the countertop of the small bar area. He walked back into the office to grab his jacket and put his money in the safe. He didn't want to be

1

robbed of the seventy thousand he had just made. He kept his .45 mm on his hip and wore his bulletproof vest while in the number house every night. The streets of North Philadelphia were not something to be taken lightly. He quickly put on his jacket and hat and turned off the light. As he walked toward the door, the two guys—now wearing ski masks—pointed guns at his forehead.

"Where the fuck is the money, old head?" one of the guys asked.

"What fucking money?" Sterling said.

They slowly forced him backward into the office and turned the light back on.

"You know what money. Where is the fucking safe?" asked the other guy.

"You must not know who you're fucking with," Sterling said.

He reached for his gun as one of the guys pushed him against the wall. Sterling pulled it out quickly. Pop, pop, pop! Sterling shot one of the attackers twice in the chest and once in the middle of the head. Bright-red blood gushed all over the walls in the office, and the man fell to the floor. The other guy pulled the ski mask off and revealed a scar on the right side of his face that ran from his ear to his chin. He pointed the gun at Sterling, who was now lying on the floor. Pop, pop! He shot Sterling in the chest.

"You killed my brother!" the guy screamed at Sterling, who lay on the floor.

He dragged his brother into the hall and then turned the office upside down to look for the safe, which Sterling hid behind a painting on the wall.

"Jackpot!" the guy said. He found two kilos of cocaine in an old refrigerator.

He put the small bundles wrapped in electrical tape up both arms of his hoodie.

He threw his brother over his shoulder and headed toward the front door. But he heard fumbling in the office, so he crept back down the hall. Sterling lay on his stomach on the floor and dialed the phone.

"No you don't, motherfucker!" the guy said.

He shot Sterling in the back of the head three times.

The hollow-tipped bullets made his head explode as fragments from his brain and skull spattered all over the wall.

"Sterling!" screamed a voice from the phone.

The guy covered his hand with his sleeve and picked up the receiver.

"He's dead, Miss," he said calmly.

"Oh my God—no!" She screamed.

The guy looked around outside the front door to make sure no one was there. It was a cold night at the end of October. He put his brother over his shoulder again and put him in the backseat of the car they had stolen earlier that day. He dropped his brother off at the emergency room, and the brother was pronounced dead on arrival. The guy who lived never spoke of what happened that night to anyone.

Ms. Sandy immediately called the cops. They found Sterling dead at the number house, but they never found his shooter. Big Sterling, also known as Starks, was the father of five grown kids and a teenager. He was in good shape for a forty-six-year-old at six foot four and a solid build. Sterling was half-black and half-Hispanic, with a good head of hair, brown skin, and almond-shaped brown eyes. He took care of his health by going to the gym. He got his reputation at the early age of fifteen, when he got his first gun, a .38 special. He killed a known drug dealer in broad daylight for trying to embarrass him. This gave him respect on the streets and turned him into a monster. He had a fuck-the-world attitude—robbing, shooting, and killing were his specialties. He met Ms. Sandy and had his first baby by her at the age of seventeen. Ms. Sandy was put out on the streets after her crack-addicted mother was evicted. Sterling knew he had to take care of Ms. Sandy and his new daughter, and Ms. Sandy always talked about having a home of her own. Big Sterling hustled crack cocaine on the North Philadelphia streets until he was able to purchase a three-story home for his family. He paid for the house in cash and fixed it up. Ms. Sandy had four more kids, one after another. They both hustled drugs to continue to provide for their growing family. Big Sterling became a beast in the street. He exposed his children to murder and mayhem at an early age. He eventually bought another three-story building, where he rented out the second and third floors and opened a number house on the first floor. The old heads in the neighborhood hung out, shot pool, and played street lottery. The only furniture was a pool table, an old oak bar he put together himself, old bar stools with vinyl seats, and mirrors on the wall behind the bar. The brightest light was over the register, and the brown commercial carpeting was worn and needed to be cleaned. One sixty-inch flat-screen TV hung on the wall. He made decent money from the small business and selling weight on the street. Sterling always said he would die in the streets, but he hated not knowing when it would be.

Two weeks after Big Sterling's funeral, the Savages met with the family lawyer to divide the $100,000 life insurance policy. Sandy and Sterling had six children: Shayla, twenty-nine; Shanice, twenty-eight; Silas, twenty-seven; Shante, twenty-six;

Shakira, twenty-five; and Little Sterling, fifteen. Big Sterling had designated $40,000 to be given to his wife and $10,000 to each child. There was another policy that gave $25,000 to Shayla and $50,000 to Little Sterling, to be paid after his enrollment in college. The reading of the will was short, as he didn't leave much. The number house went to Ms. Sandy, and she immediately closed it down. The Savage sisters were mad at each other, as usual. This time, they disagreed about their father's funeral arrangements. Sterling was Muslim, and although he wasn't on his deen, Shanice and Shakira felt that he should have had a Janazah. Shayla and Shante felt he should have a service at a funeral home.

"So he left Shayla and Sterling extra money but not us?" Shanice said as they walked out of the lawyer's office.

"Don't be so ungrateful. He didn't have to leave you anything," Silas said.

"What's the problem now?" Ms. Sandy said.

"Daddy had favorites?" Shanice asked.

"Your grandmother opened that policy when Shayla was born, and your father kept up payment on it after his mother died," Ms. Sandy said.

"So Grandmom got favorites, huh? I wish that old hag was still alive so I could give her a piece of my mind," Shanice said as they got out of the elevator.

"You are an ungrateful bitch! I just lost my husband—my best friend—and you're bitching about money!" Ms. Sandy slapped Shanice as hard as she could in the face.

"I was just saying . . . Why the fuck you have to hit me?

"You didn't even like the lady," Shakira said.

"You said enough," Shante said.

"I should slap the shit out of you, you bitch!" Shayla said, charging toward her sister.

"I haven't said enough, you ugly bitch, after how y'all buried my daddy at a fucking church, knowing he was Muslim. You ain't my fucking sister—you don't even look like us!" Shanice yelled.

Silas grabbed Shayla as she charged at Shanice again.

"Fuck you, you bum-ass bitch! That's why you ain't got shit," Shayla said.

"Whatever, bitch. You know I will fuck you up! Silas, please, let her go!" Shanice yelled in the lobby.

Ms. Sandy walked away with Shayla and Shante.

"Yeah, go ahead, Mommy. Take her side, like you always do," Shanice said.

Shanice hated that their mother always chose Shayla's side. Shayla was the oldest and the one who could do no wrong. "Let's just go," Shakira said to Shanice.

Shante and Shayla drove Ms. Sandy home, and Shakira took Shanice to calm her down. They always paired up that way. Silas loved his sisters but hated the drama and decided to keep out of the argument. Little Sterling was quiet and went with the flow. He hated when his sisters fought and loved them all differently. The big three-story house felt cold and quiet as Shayla and Ms. Sandy walked in. Everything was new: the dark hardwood floors, bay windows, marble countertops, and stainless steel appliances in the kitchen as well as fresh white paint on the walls and plush black carpet upstairs. Sterling had a lot of work done on the house. He always said that he couldn't buy a mansion, but he wanted his wife to live like a queen. Ms. Sandy kept her home spotless, even with her many grandchildren who often visited.

"You can still smell him in here," Ms. Sandy said as she walked in.

He usually sat in the brown leather recliner and watched their sixty-five-inch TV. She teared up as she took off her coat and sat in his chair.

"Mom, come on and eat before you get sick," Shayla said.

Shayla fixed her mother a plate of leftover spaghetti. Ms. Sandy hadn't eaten much in the past few days. Ms. Sandy sat at the table in a complete daze, and Shayla sat across from her. She had never seen her mother so sad. She had seen her mother and father fight hard, but she had seen them love even harder.

"Mom, are you okay?" Shayla asked.

"No, baby, I am not okay. I am so sad. What am I going to do now?" She began to cry hard, and the tears ran down her cheeks.

Shayla sat at the table and consoled her mother and cried with her. Little Sterling walked in, and he began to cry too. They held each other at the kitchen table. Things would not be the same in the Savage family, and they knew it.

Chapter 2

Shanice

Shanice was a small-framed girl with brown skin, a pretty face, and light-brown eyes. Her black hair hung to her mid back, but she always wore weaves. She took after her father's side of the family, which was half-black and half-Hispanic. She had a small waist with hips and a big butt that she inherited from her mother's side. She dressed to impress, and she kept her kids in name brands. She was the troublemaker in the family. Her three boys—Corrie, age seven; Trezvon, age five; and Tyreek, age three—were known as the bad asses in the family. Shanice rarely cared what came out of her mouth. On the streets, she was known for fighting, among other things. Girls knew not to fuck with her or her sisters. She would argue with her sisters and fight for them the same day. She showed her boys love by beating them, calling them names, and cursing at them. She always said it made them tough.

"How the fuck he gonna leave Shayla more money than us?" Shanice asked Shakira.

"This shit is crazy. Y'all are always fighting," Shakira said.

"What did Shante say?" Shanice asked.

"She ain't say shit. You know she always plays neutral but takes Shayla side." Shakira replied.

"I fucking can't stand Shayla. That bitch is always trying to act like she's so goody-goody. I know Mommy don't like me, and every chance she gets, she calls me out and hits me. One day, I am going to knock her the fuck out when she hits me," Shanice said.

"You are crazy. Mommy will break your neck. I usually stick with you, but that's one time I won't," Shakira said.

"Damn, it's like that, Sis?" Shanice said.

"That's our fucking mom. She's tripping, but so are you," Shakira said.

"You want me to take you to get the kids?" Shanice asked.

"No, Steven's here," Shakira said as they pulled up to her house.

"Where are you going?" Shakira asked.

"I am about to get this money from Trez. I will call you later," Shanice said.

She pulled up on the corner, and Trez walked over to her 2001 white Chevy Impala. Trez was five foot nine, with dark and wavy hair, thick lashes and eyebrows, a mustache, and dark skin. He went to the gym, and it showed. He jumped into her car while text-messaging someone. He wore a white polo thermal, a pair of dark denim jeans, and a fresh pair of Timberlands.

"What's up?" she said.

"You're looking good. Where are you coming from?" Trez said, admiring her black, fishnet stockings and black Yves Saint Laurent sweater dress that came to her knees as well as leather YSL knee boots and a leather jacket to match.

"We went to the lawyer's office to see what my dad left for us. Me and Shay almost fought," she said, trying to spark conversation.

"What did he leave you?" he asked.

"A little: three thousand dollars." She lied, knowing that he would try to take most of her money to buy drugs, flip it, and leave her with nothing.

"I know I get half, right?" he said, smiling.

"Yeah, you know I've got you when the check comes, but I need money now. I need gas, I want to get my hair and nails done, and the boys need a haircut," she whined.

He pulled a knot of money out of his pocket and gave her two hundred-dollar bills. "That's it? I wanted to get a full weave," she said.

"You'd better go to the Dominicans. What the fuck do you keep getting weaves for? I like my bitches to have real hair," he said as he answered his phone.

"Bitches?" she said, confused.

"Call me later," he said as he jumped out the car and went on with his phone conversation.

"Who the fuck are you talking to?" she said, jumping out of the car and following him.

"You go ahead with that crazy shit," he said, jumping in his black 2010 Tahoe, which was parked in front of her car.

"I heard a bitch voice on the other end," she said, running toward his truck.

Shanice picked up a brick and threw it at his windshield, almost cracking it. He got back out of the truck.

"Go home, Shanice, before I fuck you up out here," he said after telling the voice on the phone he would call back.

"Who the fuck were you on the phone with?" She stood in front of his car with another brick.

"I will bust your shit up. Try me!" she yelled.

Trez ran toward Shanice and slapped her across the face. She threw the brick at him, but he dodged it. He punched her in the face hard as she hit the ground. Trez grabbed Shaniece by the hair and dragged her back to her car. This scraped up her legs and exposed her as her dress flew up. He dropped her on the curb and slapped her face again. Then he stomped on her hand as hard as he could. He opened the car door and slammed her head into it. Trez picked her up and threw her in the car.

"Bitch, go the fuck home before I really fuck you up!" he said.

Shanice grabbed her hand and screamed in pain. When Trez put his head in the car and tried to bite her face, Shanice pulled a can of pepper spray off her key ring and sprayed him in the eyes.

"I can't fucking see!" he screamed.

She got the small pocketknife she kept under the seat and stabbed him in the leg three times.

"Fucking bitch just stabbed me!" he yelled, holding his eyes and his right leg. She slammed her car door and started her car. Trez's sister, Tiffany, ran down the street to see what was going on.

"What the fuck did you do to her? You are so fucking stupid. You gonna get locked up," Tiffany yelled at Trez.

"You want me to take you home?" Tiffany asked, opening the passenger door.

"Nah, I am good," Shaniece said, pulling off before Tiffany could close the door and get out of the street.

"That bitch just stabbed me with a knife!" Trez yelled at Tiffany and pointed at his leg. He limped behind Shanice's car as she pulled away.

Chapter 3

Shakira

Shakira was twenty-five years old and known as "baby girl." No one expected much from her, as she could never keep a job and depended on men for money. Ms. Sandy always thought of her as a freeloader. She always looked for a hustle to pay her bills. Her three children, all by different fathers, were Cameron, seven years old; Dallas, five years old; and Gizelle, three months old. She had a pretty face with brown skin and brown eyes. Her gut was from having three C-sections. She frequently dyed her shoulder-length hair dark blonde. She frequently borrowed clothes from her sisters or friends or stole what she wanted because she couldn't afford it. She had big breasts, and her butt and hips were average.

"Where the fuck have you been all day?" Steven asked Shakira as she walked in the door. He sat on the couch, smoking a blunt.

"I told you I was going to the lawyer's office," she said.

Steven and Shakira had been together for three years on and off. She recently gave birth to one of his many children. She took her coat off with a confused look on her face as she noticed her house was as cold as it was outside.

"The heat stopped working," Steven said.

"Can you check it out for me?" she asked.

"I don't have time for that. I need to make a move. What did you do with the three grand I told you to hold?" he asked.

"It's upstairs," she said.

"Go get it," he demanded as he looked in the refrigerator.

"Damn, you ain't got food or heat. That's fucked up," he added.

"You find that funny? You do know your daughter is here, right?" Shakira replied.

"Man, just go get my paper so I can handle this business," he said.

She ran upstairs to get the money out of the safe in her closet.

"I took out forty dollars to get Gizelle some Pampers. I was going to put it back when I got my next check," she said hesitantly as she came down the steps.

"Who the fuck told you to spend my money?" he yelled.

"Your daughter needed diapers," she said.

"Fuck all that shit. That was my fucking money. You should have used your check for that," he said.

"Can you pick me up a heater? It's going to get really cold tonight, and I don't want the kids to get sick," she said.

"I don't have any money for that," he replied, counting his money.

"Well, can you at least take me by my aunt's to get the kids?" she asked.

"I got shit to do. You done fucked up my money. I ain't doing shit for you, fucking bitch," he said as he slammed the door.

Shakira opened the door and yelled, "You selfish bitch—fuck you!"

"You're gonna be cold tonight," he said, laughing as he got into his truck and left.

Shakira began to cry. She called Shanice, who did not answer her phone. Shakira almost asked Shayla if she could borrow some money, but she knew Shayla would refuse. She thought about calling her mother, but she didn't want to burden her or give her the chance to ask where the kids' fathers were. She called Steven, but he did not answer.

She called her aunt Nancy to ask if the kids could stay the night, and she agreed.

Shakira only had forty-five dollars to her name until she got paid in a few days, so it would be a long stretch to buy a small heater. So she put pots of hot water on the stove, and turned on her oven and tried to warm her house the best she could.

Chapter 4

Shante

Shante was known as "Miss Perfect." She was the only one of her sisters that was married, and they envied her for that. Shante was twenty-six years old, but she could pass for an eighteen-year-old. She had chestnut-brown eyes and a small waist, while her breasts, her butt, and her hips were big. She wore her hair long and all natural, with blonde streaks. She didn't care much about dressing in designer labels but had a few. She was usually patient, but her patience with the man she married was wearing thin. Shante had been married to Harold for three years and had been with him since high school. She had expected that being married would make their relationship better, but it only made things worse. By their second year of marriage, he had a baby on the side that was eighteen months old. He cheated, returned home whenever he wanted, and talked to Shante disrespectfully. He argued that he paid all the bills, so he could do as he pleases. Shante was furious with him when he started this behavior. Harold said he knew Shante was cheating because so many men checked for her. One night when she went out with her sisters, he got so jealous that he slapped her to the floor and spit on her after a heated argument. Shante waited until he was in a deep sleep, and then she boiled a pot of water. She threw it on him and then beat him with an extension cord. He suffered second-degree burns, and the welts never fully went away. He thought about pressing charges, but he didn't want to be embarrassed by the situation. When her father found out what was happening, he had picked Harold up one night when he got off work with Silas. Big Sterling put an unloaded shotgun in Harold's mouth and pulled the trigger. He scared him so bad that he shit his pants. Sterling told his son-in-law that if he ever laid hands on Shante again, he would blow his head off. Shante and Harold didn't talk for months after that. Harold was beginning to act like his old self again since her father had died, and Shante knew a storm was about to erupt.

Shante had a long day after coming home from the lawyer's office. Her kids, Morgan, Mathew, Megan, and Mya, were stairsteps, from age five to eight. After dinner, they all agreed on watching *Diary of a Wimpy Kid* together. She made popcorn as she watched highlights from the basketball game at the school where she was an assistant teacher. She smiled as she texted Jared.

"Great game!" she texted him.

"Thanks! It would be even better if I could see you tonight," he replied.

"We can meet up Thursday for dinner, once Harold comes home," she sent back.

"I miss your kisses," he wrote.

"XOXOXO see you in the morning," she texted in return.

She heard the key turn, and she knew Harold was drunk. He got off at five thirty in the evening, and it was now seven forty-five. He walked in with his city uniform on. He was tall and dark with a clean beard and a belly that was bloated from all the beer and his diabetes. Shante put the popcorn in a bowl as the kids ran to greet their dad. He gave them a pack of cookies as he followed Shante into the kitchen.

"How was your day?" she asked.

"It was all right," he answered as he put a six-pack of Coors Light in the refrigerator.

"I put your dinner in the microwave," she said as she brought the bowl of popcorn into the living room. The doorbell rang, and Shante answered. A brown-skinned woman in a nursing uniform, holding a snotty-nosed and nappy-headed little girl, asked for Harold.

"Who are you?" Shante asked.

"Harold knows," the woman said.

Harold walked to the door and moved Shante to the side.

"Who is this Miss Gonorrhea with the baby?" Shante said, pushing Harold out of the way. Harold pushed Shante into the house and closed the door.

He had never brought his mess home before. He usually hid it until Shante found out. She didn't find out about the baby he had on the side until the woman was going into labor and couldn't reach him, so she sent a friend to his mother's house to find him, and Shante was there. Shante listened as Harold told the woman who showed up at the door that he couldn't watch the baby for her. Instead, he gave her money to pay her sister for watching the baby. Shante paced back and forth in the kitchen until Harold came back in the house.

"So you're just going to let this bitch come to our home, where our kids are, with that little rug rat?" Shante said, holding her hand on her hip.

"How many times have I told you? I pay the bills here, and I do what the fuck I want. Don't ask me shit," he said.

"You mean to tell me that we are married, and you openly cheat on me and throw it in my face, and it's okay?" she asked.

"When you put your name on a house, you can do what you want in your own shit. You're basically here on borrowed time because of the kids," he said.

Shante had heard this many times before. She had had enough of Harold. She looked at him and wondered how she could kill him and get away with it. She laughed, knowing it could be arranged.

"You know what? You're right. I am going into the living room to watch a movie with my kids."

"My fucking living room, bitch!" he yelled.

"Miss Bitch to you, you sorry-ass bastard," she yelled back.

Shante contemplated how she would get out of her failed marriage. The $10,000 from her dad was coming right on time. Shante went to bed after the movie with the kids. Harold fell asleep on the couch, as usual. She hadn't had sex with him in ten months, since she found out she had gonorrhea at her last clinic visit. She met Jared before she started teaching. He was a senior, and he had lied about his age, so she kept their relationship a secret. She told him everything about her and Harold. Jared was mature for his age, and he became Shante's best friend— something her husband hadn't been in a long time. She grew to really care about him over the past five months, and he treated her well. He had his own apartment, so she usually met with him after work a few times per week. He did things to her that no eighteen-year-old should know how to do. She didn't feel like she was cheating on her husband, because he had cheated on her first. She had no idea where her relationship with Jared would go. All she knew was that he made her feel good, and she loved that.

Chapter 5

Shayla

Shayla was twenty-nine and the oldest of Sterling and Sandy's children. She took care of all her siblings. She had no children and was known for having her shit together. She kept a good job. Shayla was dark-skinned, with big hips and thighs. Shayla took after her mother and was a little darker than her sisters. She always wore a long weave. Her eyes were lighter than her sisters' eyes. Her face was covered with acne scars, but she always looked good and wore name brand clothes.

Shayla answered her prepaid flip phone, and a voice said, "You have a call from Hick at Curran-Fromhold Correctional Facility. To accept, please press five."

Shayla pressed five.

"Hello," she said.

"What's up?" Hick said.

"Getting ready for work," she answered.

"How was the meeting at the lawyer's office?"

"It was cool. Everybody got ten grand. My mom is not taking it too well, so my aunt is staying with her to keep her company."

"Oh. Did you talk to my lawyer?" he asked.

"Yeah, I gave him some more money, but he wants ten thousand more," she said.

"Well, just pay that after this next run. They fed us some bullshit for dinner tonight. I wish I could have some jerked chicken, baked macaroni, and cabbage. That sounds good."

"As soon as you come home, I will make you some," she promised.

"They're about to cut the phones off. I will call you tomorrow," he said.

"I love you," she said.

"One," he said brushing her off. She hung up and finished ironing her uniform. She stopped to pick up some food from the Caribbean restaurant not far from her job.

"Savage!" called the correctional officer said as she walked in CFCF prison. The officer patted her down, and checked her food for contraband.

"What's up?" she said.

"How have you been? I thought you be out longer," the officer said.

"I tried to stay home, but I can't. My mom is taking it harder than the rest of us," she said, taking off her jacket. She looked at the board for her assignment.

"You like overnight?" he said.

"Not really. I just picked up a few shifts for extra money," she said, clocking in.

"See you later," he said. She made her way to D-Two-Three, where she and her coworker Diamond met up. Diamond was also Shayla's best friend. They had grown up together.

"Hey, girl," Diamond said.

"What's up?" Shayla said.

"You ready to count?" Diamond asked.

"Yeah, let's get it over with." They counted the inmates and made sure all the cells were locked.

"Cell thirty-two is out for shower clean-up tonight," Diamond said.

"Can I go first?" Shayla asked, even though it was Diamond's week to go first.

"Yeah, go ahead. I'm mad at this nigga. His baby mama was talking some shit in the shop about him coming home and them getting married," Diamond said.

"What! Get the fuck out of here," Shayla said.

"Yes, girl, so this pussy is off limits," Diamond said, laughing.

Shayla made her way to cell thirty-two, let out one inmate, and then pretended to lock the door before she walked into the cell. Diamond took the other inmate to the showers to start his job.

"Hey, baby," she said as she went into the cell and gave him the food from the restaurant. Hick embraced her and gave her a kiss. He was about six foot three and built like a football player. He was brown-skinned and had brown eyes, a bald head, and a full beard. They kissed each other passionately as he caressed her butt and unzipped her pants. She knelt down and unzipped his pants. She pulled his hard, thick penis out and teased the head with her tongue, giving it wet kisses and then devouring it. She stroked his penis with her mouth until he could take no more. He pulled her up off of her knees, pulled her pants down, turned her over, and put himself inside of her. He pounded her from behind until he exploded inside of her.

"You all right?" he asked.

"I will be when you come home," she said, out of breath.

"Me too," he said. She cleaned herself with some baby wipes as he ate his food.

"You know the pickup is Friday," he said. "See if you can talk to this nigga so we can get a contact number. I hate the fact that I don't know this clown."

"How did you link up with him?" she asked.

"It was Kyree's brother Boo connect. Before he got rocked, he took me around with him, and I got familiar with the workers. When he died, I had never met his connect. I took Boo phone from his crib. The connect always calls the phone when it's pick up time," he explained.

They kissed each other, and Shayla went back to work. Diamond went to meet with her boyfriend but only to give him a piece of her mind. Shayla locked them into his cell.

"So are you getting married?" Diamond asked.

"Yo, stop with your nonsense," Jermaine said.

He grabbed her and kissed her. She fought it but finally gave in.

"What's up with your people?" he asked. "Sounds like they get a lot of work."

"I don't know what you're talking about," she said.

"You need to see what your girl is into so we can get this money," he said.

"I am not worried about that. I get my own money," she said.

"You want us to be together without me being in the streets all night, right?" he asked.

"Yeah, but I want you to get a job," she said.

"I hate to tell you this, but I am always going to be a hustler," he said.

Diamond thought about it.

"I am doing this to take care of you," he said.

"Okay, I will let you know," she said, signaling for Shayla to open the cell door.

Shayla and Diamond looked out for each other every Wednesday night. Diamond had met Jermaine five months ago. Shayla met Hick two years ago, and then he was arrested a little over a month ago for conspiracy to commit a homicide. It looked like he would beat the case. She had been working for the prison for five years and decided that if they didn't know she was with him, why tell them? They saw each other every week and talked every day on her prepaid phone. Before he got locked up, the relationship was falling apart. He was doing the unthinkable on the streets while she held him together through thick and thin. When he got locked up, he needed her to move his coke on the streets and keep his connects in pocket. She did whatever he wanted, moving a lot of it through the jail and dropping it off to his people in the street. She always took her cut off the top, and she put his money in an account. It was very easy because no one expected she was doing it.

Chapter 6

Shakira

The heater had been out for almost five days at Shakira's house, and it was freezing inside. She made a pallet of blankets for the kids on the kitchen floor by the oven. She cried as she called Gazelle's father, Steven, hoping he would bring them a space heater until she could get the regular one fixed. She tried to contact Shanice, but she didn't want to burden her after the incident with Trez. Shakira was renting from a slum lord. Everything needed to be fixed, and he usually didn't fix anything. The rent was $400 a month, which she could afford with her welfare check and her son Cameron's Supplemental Security Income (SSI) check for behavioral issues. Her living room furniture consisted of two worn, black leather sofas and a thirty-two-inch TV that sat on the coffee table. There was a small wooden table with four chairs in the small dining area. The house had one empty bedroom and a middle room that held an old twin bed. Her room had a full-sized bed with an old crib and a nineteen-inch TV.

"Hello, can you please call me? It's an emergency," she said, leaving the twentieth message on Steven's phone.

She finally gave up. It was three forty-five in the morning, and she needed sleep. She lay down on the floor with the baby next to her and fell asleep with the other children. Later, she was awakened by a loud knock at the door.

"Who is it?" she yelled.

"It's the gas company," a man's voice said.

She opened the door in her coat.

"We came to shut your gas off unless you are able to make a payment immediately," he said.

"Please, sir, I don't have any heat as it is, and I have three kids," she pleaded with tears in her eyes. She opened the door for him to look inside. He saw the baby in a full snowsuit begin to cry and the boys looking toward the door with their coats on.

"It's the last day for shutoffs before winter." He handed her paperwork with information on assistance with paying utility bills.

"Try to take care of this before spring rolls in," he said.

"Thank you so much," she said, closing the door.

"I am hungry!" Cameron and Dallas cried together.

"Okay," Shakira said.

She looked in the fridge, which was almost empty. But she had plenty of cereal and milk, thanks to the WIC program. She made her boys each a bowl of Kix cereal, and she fed the baby formula mixed with rice cereal.

Knock, knock, knock!

"What the fuck now?" she mumbled. "Who is it?" she yelled.

"Can we take a look at your heater? It's the gas company," the worker yelled back from outside.

"I don't have any money," she said, opening the door.

"It's okay," he replied.

The two workers went to her basement and fixed the heater within an hour. Shakira and her kids felt heat coming from the vents again. As the workers came upstairs, Shakira was crying with happiness.

"I don't know how to thank you enough. I have been without heat for five days," she said.

"Your thanks are enough," the worker said as he teared up too.

The baby could finally sleep in her crib, and the boys were able to walk around the house without their coats. Right after the gas company left, Ms. Sandy knocked on the front door. She walked in and took her coat off as she went to the dining room table, and put her pocketbook down.

"Why haven't you called me?" Ms. Sandy said.

"I have been busy," Shakira replied.

"You're too busy to check on your mother?" she asked.

"I thought Shayla was with you," Shakira said.

"She was, but I expected to see you more, considering you live around the corner," Ms. Sandy explained. "You've been too busy chasing that bum. Your heat has been off for a week, and he hasn't been here, I heard."

"What, did you come here just to dump on me?" Shakira complained.

"No, I came to see you and the kids and to help you out if you need it. Maybe you have too much pride to ask for a hand from me, but you should have dropped the kids off at my house instead of making them suffer. I've had to hear the shit from your aunt Nancy. You know I hate that," she said.

"As you can see, the heat works," Shakira said.

"I'm going to cook a really big dinner for Thanksgiving," Ms. Sandy said as she looked in the refrigerator. "Where's the food? You didn't get stamps yet?" she added.

"I get them today. I have to check my card," Shakira said, grabbing her phone.

"Where are the kids? Dallas, Cameron!" Ms. Sandy yelled up the steps.

The boys ran downstairs.

"Mom, you're going to wake up Gazelle," Shakira said, annoyed.

"I wanna see her too," Ms. Sandy said. She kissed the boys and gave them each a bag of brownies out of her oversized Coach bag.

"Mom, are you going to be here for a while? I want to go to the market," Shakira said.

"Yeah, I will stay with the kids. I needed to get out of that house," Ms. Sandy said.

The Philadelphia welfare system would cut someone off in a heartbeat, so Shakira was happy that she got her food stamps and cash. She still had to wait for her son's SSI check to come in the mail. She grabbed a pen and jotted down the bills that she needed to pay: electricity, rent, phone, and gas. She added up her odds and ends for the kids' haircuts. They also needed sneakers and jackets. She shook her head as she thought about what she wasn't going to pay right now. Since she had until spring to sort out the gas statement and she could get help, she decided to get clothes for the boys. She pulled her hair into a ponytail and jumped in the shower. When she was done, she put on her dark-denim True Religion jeans and a black long-sleeved shirt. She put on her black hoodie, a black leather jacket, and a pair of black Uggs. As she went downstairs, she grabbed the baby and gave her to Ms. Sandy, who had made herself comfortable on the couch.

"I am going to catch the bus to Save-A-Lot and then get a hack back," Shakira said.

As she sat on the bus, she called Steven again.

"Hello!" she said, surprised that he answered.

"What's up?" he said, sounding as if he had just woken up.

"I have been calling you for five days! The kids and I have been in the cold," she said.

"What? My phone's been acting up. I didn't get your messages," he said.

"Why haven't you called me, Steven?" she yelled.

"Where are you?" he asked, changing the topic.

"On my way to the market," she answered.

"What market?" he asked.

"Save-A-Lot on Twenty-Ninth and Dauphin," she said.

"Did you get your heat fixed?" he asked.

"Yeah," she said.

"You want me to pick you up when you're done?" he asked.

"Yeah, that would be nice," she said.

"All right. Call me," he said.

Shakira forgot about the fact that he had walked out on her and her kids when they needed him most. Now she just wanted to get to the market and shop before he changed his mind. An hour later, she called Steven, and he was there within minutes. He even helped her put the bags in the trunk of his Escalade. Steven was a drug dealer, but he was not very good at it. He often got robbed, he didn't save money, and he was a softy. Shakira had a soft heart when it came to him. He had four children, not including Gazelle. Standing six foot two, he had played a little college ball in Arizona before he got kicked out for selling weed and having poor grades. The neighborhood girls loved his good looks. He still lived with his mother, and she still took care of him.

"So where have you been?" Shakira asked.

"I was in Camden with my people, taking care of some business," Steven replied.

"You still could have called," she said.

"You missed me?" he said, smiling.

"Yeah, can't you tell?" she said.

"Can I have a kiss?" he answered.

As he stopped at the light, she leaned over and gave him a deep kiss. He turned the music up loud, blasting Trey Songz's "Last Time." When they got to Shakira's house, he parked in front and took a call. Shakira got the bags out of the truck as he talked on the phone. When she looked out the front door after carrying the bags in, he was gone. She called him, and there was no answer. She was pissed that he didn't even come in and see the baby. Cameron and Dallas were playing upstairs noisily. Shakira ignored them at first as she put the food away. But after she yelled at them to stop and they didn't, she decided she couldn't take it anymore. She ran upstairs took off her belt, and beat both the boys. They screamed loudly.

"What the fuck are you beating them for?" Ms. Sandy yelled from downstairs.

"They were making too much noise," Shakira screamed back at her.

"They're being fucking kids. Take that shit out on the nigga you mad at," Ms. Sandy said.

"You better get out of my face," Shakira said.

"Bitch, I will knock you the fuck out!" Ms. Sandy yelled as she made a fist to warn her daughter. Ms. Sandy was a medium-built, heavy-handed, five foot four, dark-skinned woman. People said she and Shayla looked alike. She had whooped a few asses, and her daughters knew not to mess with her.

"If you beat them like that again, for nothing, I will knock you out," Ms. Sandy said. Shakira was angry because she always got tough love from her mom. She grabbed her hoodie and went to her girlfriend Mika's house, around the corner. Mika answered the door, talking on the phone, so Shakira walked in and made herself at home. Mika was an around-the-way hairstylist. She sold pills, weed, and juice out of her house. She was Silas's baby mama. She had one of the nicest houses in the neighborhood, and she actually owned it. She was hood rich, and she took care of Silas.

"I got some new exotic shit in. You want to try it?" Mika asked when she finished on the phone.

"I ain't got money for that," Shakira said.

Mika passed her a blunt, and Shakira took a drag.

"This is nice," Shakira said, inhaling hard.

"I told you. Why don't you buy this pound off of me? We can go to a college party tonight, and you can sell most of it there. You'll get your money back in a few hours," Mika said.

"I am so scared of that shit," Shakira answered.

"Bitch, what've you got to lose? It's just weed," Mika said. "I will front it to you, so you can bag this shit up and give me a stack in a week. I will be selling pills and juice at the party tonight, so the weed is all yours. I just want to see you get some money," Mika explained.

Shakira grabbed the pound of weed. She was tired of being broke and having so many bills and things she wanted to do for the kids and herself.

"I need something to wear tonight," she said.

"No, you don't. We're getting in and out," Mika said, taking another drag. "Here, smoke this with me. We can bag up together. Mix it up with nicks and dubs if you want, but they usually buy dimes and dubs on campus. Save the nicks for these bum-ass niggas around the way," Mika added.

They were done in an hour, so Shakira decided to go home and check on the kids before going to the party. She took the weed with her and stashed it in the safe in her room. She had bought the safe as a gift for Steven, but he never used it, so she reset the keypad with her own code. Her mother had fixed the kids dinner, and she was cleaning the house.

"Cameron's check came," Ms. Sandy said, passing it to Shakira. "I am going to stay here tonight and go home tomorrow. They've been shooting around there, and Sterling is away at a basketball clinic."

Shakira was fine with that because she needed a babysitter. A phone call from an unknown number made Shakira's phone ring.

"Hello!" she said.

"Why the fuck you keep calling Steven?" said the voice of a woman on the other end.

"Who is this?" Shakira said.

"Don't worry about that. But I am ready to have his baby, and we're together now," she said.

"Well, get in line with the rest of us. He doesn't take care of his kids. Do you think you're gaining something? All you're getting is a bunch of problems. Congratulations!" Shakira said.

"Bitch, you just mad 'cause he don't want to be with you," the caller said.

"No, I'm mad because I can't beat your ass right now," Shakira said, hanging up as tears rolled down her cheek. She lay down on her bed and fell asleep as she listened to a Mary J. Blige album. She woke up to Mika's phone call at nine forty-five that night.

"I am getting ready to come scoop you up," Mika said.

Shakira quickly fixed her hair and put on a little eyeliner. Mika pulled up in a black Tahoe, blasting "Juicy" by Biggie Smalls. Shakira ran downstairs, yelling to her mom that she would be back later.

"Did you bring enough?" Mika asked.

"I brought half of it out," Shakira said.

"Here's a blunt. You're going to light it at the party, and they will ask where you got the weed," Mika explained.

The party was off campus, in a big house. They walked in like they belonged and both grabbed drinks. People were smoking all over the party. Shakira lit her blunt and passed it to a student to try, just like Mika suggested. The guy took a long pull and then inhaled.

"This is nice. Where you get this shit?" he asked.

Shakira pointed to herself.

"What you got?"

"Dimes."

"Let me get four," he requested.

Shakira dug out four bags as he gave her two twenty-dollar bills. She moved through the party and continued to sell until her supply was gone. She went to a bathroom and closed the door to count the money and put it away, but she wished she had brought more to the party with her. She was so happy that she would be able to pay all of her bills and buy some things for herself. She put half of the money she owed Mika to the side. She would also have enough money to take the kids to get some clothes and sneakers. Shakira and Mika mingled the rest of the night, taking down the students' phone numbers and learning about upcoming parties. Shakira was excited that she had clientele. She knew she would be able to get rid of the rest of the weed and maybe buy some more before her $10,000 inheritance payment came.

Chapter 7

Shanice

Shanice put an ice pack on her hand, which had been throbbing for a week now. The doctor told her it wasn't broken, just strained. She continued to take the Percocet they gave her and her own Xanax and syrup to sleep through the pain from the injury and from not knowing where Trez was. He hadn't called her since the incident, and she was beyond upset.

"Mommy, I am hungry," Tyreek said, bursting into her room.

"Leave me alone, 'Reek. Wait a fuckin' minute!" she yelled.

"I wanna eat now, you fuckin' bitch," he yelled back.

"What the fuck you say?" She jumped up and spanked him with a belt.

"You motherfucker! Don't cuss at me like that again. You eat when I feel like cooking," she said.

Tyreek screamed to the top of his lungs as he threw his toys against the wall. Tyreek looked just like Trez, and he had a mean streak and behavioral problems. He had seen and heard a lot for his young age.

"I need a fucking blunt," Shanice yelled.

She called her neighborhood friend, Stacy, and asked her over to drink and smoke a blunt. She settled the kids in their room with pizza and video games. Shanice, Stacy, and Stacy's two cousins sat at the dining room table, smoking weed and playing cards. Shanice lived in a newly developed Philadelphia Housing Authority apartment. Her apartment contained black leather furniture and glass tables in the living room and dining area. She had a full wall of mirrors as well as a fifty-inch plasma screen TV mounted on another wall. There were wooden bunk beds in the kids' room, and her bedroom held a king-sized bed with a leather headboard. Her kids had made dents and small holes in the wall, but everyone in her neighborhood thought it was the nicest home there.

"Why didn't you bring your kids over?" Shanice asked.

"They're at my mom's house. What happened with Trez again?" Stacy asked.

"He caught me talking to this dude and flipped the fuck out. Bitch, you should have seen me. I was scared as shit," Shanice lied, not wanting them to know he was cheating on her.

"That's crazy. He will call you, though. He always comes back to his boo," Stacy said, laughing.

"I don't know. He's been trippin' lately," Shanice said, still nursing her sprained hand.

Bang, bang, bang! Someone pounded on the door.

"That's probably him, acting all crazy," Stacy said.

"Who the fuck is it?" Stacy yelled, laughing as she opened the door.

"Bitch, get the fuck on the floor!" Three guys in face masks carrying guns ran into Shanice's apartment. One guy put a gun in Stacy's face.

"Bitch, where he keep the money at?" he asked.

"What money?" Stacy said.

Shanice and the other two women hid under the table. The men turned the house upside down but found nothing. They kicked in the door of the kids' room. They grabbed Shanice by the hair and dragged her out from under the table.

"You his bitch, ain't you? Tell that pussy that the next time I see him, he better be strapped. Nobody takes money from me," said the guy.

He took the gun and ran it up and down Shanice's body, and then he hit her in the head and face with the gun. Blood gushed from her head as she fell unconscious. The three guys ran out of the apartment, and Stacy called 911. It didn't take long for the ambulance to get there. The paramedics rushed her to the emergency room, where she was taken care of right away. Stacy told Ms. Sandy, who called the rest of the family. They rushed to her side.

Two days later, Shanice finally woke up while Shakira and Ms. Sandy were in the room.

"I have the worst fucking headache," Shanice said, confused.

She rubbed her head and noticed there was a bald spot with stitches, and she was in severe pain. She moaned a little more as she touched her face. The right side was swollen, and she had a black eye.

"Where are the boys?" she asked.

"They have been staying with Mommy. I left them with Little Sterling for today," Shakira replied.

"What happened to me?" Shanice asked.

"You were pistol-whipped," Shakira said.

"Where the fuck is Trez?" Shanice screamed.

"He hasn't called or answered his phone," Shakira answered.

"It's his fucking fault this shit happened. He robbed somebody, and they retaliated on me because I am his wifey," she said.

"Do you know who it was?" Ms. Sandy asked.

"No, they wore masks. How long am I going to be here?" she asked. Shanice was still mad at her mother for hitting her.

"You just woke up a minute ago. You gonna go chase that nigga, Trez? He doesn't give a fuck about you. Look around and see who's here for you," Ms. Sandy said.

"Mom, I really don't want to hear that shit right now."

"You know what? You're alive, whoop-dee-do. I am going the fuck home—I refuse to watch you make an ass of yourself," Ms. Sandy said.

Shanice rolled her eyes at her mother.

"You ain't left yet?" Shanice said.

Ms. Sandy stormed out, and Shakira tried to call her back.

"Are you serious, Sis? Not at a time like this," Shakira said a moment later.

"Fuck that. You can leave too. I ain't gonna let anybody talk down on my man, ya dig?" Shanice said.

Shakira left, shaking her head. Shanice grabbed the hospital phone and dialed the home phone number for Trez's mom.

"Hello, Miss Tammie. Where the fuck is Trez?" Shanice asked.

"I heard you got shot. Are you okay?" she asked in reply.

"Yeah. Where is he?" she said.

"Hold on," Trez's mother said.

Shanice heard Trez's sister tell his mom that he had company and his mother explaining who was on the phone.

"Hello, Shanice?" said his sister, taking the phone.

"Yeah?"

"Bitch, I heard what happened. You okay?"

"Yeah, but where is Trez?"

"Hold on," his sister said. After that, Trez finally got on the phone.

"Hello," he said, sounding half-asleep.

"You didn't call to check on me and make sure I was still breathing. What the fuck?" she yelled.

"How the fuck was I supposed to get at you with detectives and shit around? Do me a favor: Don't say shit. Stacy told me what happened, and I know exactly who it was. Let me take care of it, and I will call you in a couple of days. Until then, just stay at your mom's house," he said.

"If she will let me," Shanice replied.

"Whatever. Just don't go home until I say," he repeated.

Shanice knew that staying at her mom's house when she got out of the hospital would be crazy. She texted Shakira and apologized for snapping at her. Shanice felt that her mother always looked down her, so she asked Shakira if she could stay there for a couple days until Trez fixed the problem. Shakira agreed and told her to call when she was discharged. Next, Shanice called Stacy.

"What's up?" Stacy said sleepily.

"Girl, when you coming to see me? I just woke up today," Shanice said.

"How are you feeling?" Stacy asked.

"I am okay. I need a good weave, 'cause I have a bald spot from my stitches," she said. "Have you seen Trez around?" she asked.

"Yeah, he stopped by here yesterday, asking what happened. I told him everything, and he said he gonna find that nigga and kill him," Stacy answered.

"Do you know who it was?" Shanice said.

"It sounded like it was the Hawks brothers," Stacey said.

"I know Trez ain't been taking money. I have all his guns locked up, and he hasn't asked for them," Shanice said.

"That's all I heard. Let me call you back," Stacey said, trying to get off the phone.

Shanice was experiencing the worst headache she had ever had but tried to play it off as nothing. The doctors wanted to keep her a couple extra days for evaluation. She insisted on being home with her kids, and she really wanted to get home to Trez. The doctors discharged her two days later with a prescription of Percocet for the pain and scheduled a follow-up appointment to remove her stitches two weeks later. Shakira drove Shanice's car to pick her up from the hospital, and Shanice called Trez as soon as she got in the car.

"He's not answering the phone," she said with frustration.

"You want me to take you to his house?" Shakira asked.

"Yeah, but let's go to his apartment, not his mom's house," Shanice replied.

The apartment wasn't too far from the hospital, and when they pulled up, both sisters looked for Trez's truck.

"He's here—there's his truck. Park right here Shanice said.

"Wait, what the fuck is Stacy's car doing here? It's ten in the morning! There's no reason for Stacy to be at Trez's house," Shanice said. Shakira and Shanice both took their earrings off and pulled their hair back. Shanice pulled a crowbar from the trunk and grabbed her pepper spray.

"It's fuckin' on," she said, walking toward Stacy's car. She took the crowbar and broke the back window, and then she broke the front window. She took her pocketknife and gave it to Shakira, who keyed the car and flattened all four tires. Shanice took the crowbar, broke the apartment's lock, and kicked in the door.

"Who the fuck is that?" Trez yelled from the bedroom.

"Your worst fucking nightmare," Shanice yelled.

Shanice shot Trez with pepper spray before he could hit her. He fell to the floor by the closet, naked, but Shakira pushed him into the closet and locked the door. Stacy was naked in the bed. She held the sheets over her head and screamed as Shanice grabbed one foot and Shakira grabbed the other. They pulled Stacy from the bed, and she hit the floor hard. They dragged her through the apartment, and the commercial carpet burned her back. The sisters punched and kicked Stacy.

"Stop, 'Shanice." Stacy said as she braced herself.

"Bitch, you will never cross me again," Shanice said, punching Stacy in the mouth and spitting in her face.

"Get the fuck off of me!" Stacy screamed, trying to fight back.

Shanice punched Stacy in the mouth again and then in both eyes. Then she covered Stacy with pepper spray as she and Shakira pulled her down all five front steps, scraping her bare back and butt on the concrete. Stacy turned onto her side, screaming and crying. Her back was completely bloody. Shanice kicked Stacy between the legs as hard as she could, and then she picked up a brick and aimed at Stacy's head.

"Stop, bitch. No bodies today!" Shakira said, laughing.

"Fuck with somebody else's man, bitch!" Shanice said.

Shanice felt a sharp pain in her head, so she held her head until it passed. She slammed the brick into Stacy's back and then ran to the car with Shakira. They sped off as neighbors went to their doors to see what was going on. Shakira and Shanice loved to fight as a tag team.

They went to get a couple of drinks at Lilly's, a neighborhood bar. Trez called Shanice's phone while she and Shakira were at the bar.

"What the fuck do you want?" Shanice yelled into the phone.

"Yo, you tripping. She's calling the cops," he said.

"If I get locked up, you will be too," she said. "You'd better tell her not to call the police, or else I will be your worst nightmare," she said.

"I'm gonna see what I can do. But don't threaten me—you know I'm about this life," he said. "Fuck you. Don't call me anymore—we are through," she said.

"You made up a lie about being pistol-whipped and set up some fake shit," he said.

"You almost got me killed, and then you started fucking someone I called my friend. You'd just better make sure that bitch doesn't snitch, or I am going to finish her off and take my sweet revenge on you," she said before she hung up.

Trez had a stronger hand in their relationship when Shanice was off guard, but when she wanted to get to him, she did, and she continued until he surrendered. Shanice had pulled many girls out of his apartment and beat them up before, but she never thought he would fuck someone so close to her.

"I am through with him. I told this bitch so much shit about Trez and me, and she went and fucked him. I need to find out who those dudes were that ran up in my crib. I'll send them to that nigga's house. Fuck that—he gonna pay," Shanice said.

"Exactly. Fuck that nigga," Shakira said.

"I think I'd better go lie down. My head is killing me," Shanice said.

Shakira helped her to the car, took her to her house, and helped her to bed. Shanice took two Percocet pills and fell asleep in Shakira's bed. Shakira watched her sister sleep as tears rolled down her face. She wanted to kill Stacey and Trez for hurting her.

Chapter 8

Shante

Shante was up early, getting ready for work. She had slept well the night before, thinking of meeting up with Jared.

"You're still here?" Harold asked as she drank her coffee.

"Don't start your shit," she said.

"Make yourself useful—make me some breakfast," Harold said.

"You don't really want me to cook," she said.

"Make me some eggs and turkey bacon on a roll," he demanded.

"That's not how you ask," she said.

"Please? I do pay all the bills," he reminded her.

She grabbed the turkey bacon and eggs to start his requested breakfast.

"I like milk in my eggs," he said.

She grabbed the milk and milk of magnesia from the refrigerator. She mixed it together well and made him a sandwich to bring with him. She got the kids ready and left before Harold did. When she got in the car, she texted him and asked him to pick the kids up for her after school. He texted her back saying it wasn't a problem. He acted as if he hated her, but he always did what was needed for the kids. After she dropped the kids off at their school, she went on with her workday. At noon, she drove five blocks away from Franklin High School, where she worked, to meet Jared during her one-hour lunch. He got into her 2011 Tahoe, wearing Polo sweats from head to toe. He smelled so good that it turned her on. He was six foot two, light-skinned, and in great shape. He had wavy black hair.

He was toting a bag of her favorite food from the nearby Saladworks restaurant and a latte.

"How you been, cutie," he asked, kissing her.

"I'm good now," she said.

"You coming over tonight?" he asked.

"Yeah, but you know I can't stay," she said.

"As long as you can stay long enough for me to make you cum," he whispered in her ear.

"Oh yes, definitely," she said.

She got excited, wanting to have him right away. They kissed each other passionately and forgot about their food as they continued to make out in her car. They went back to school separately as if nothing had happened. The school day was soon over, and Shante went to Shakira's to see Shanice. When she opened the door, the smell of weed filled the air.

"Where are your kids?" she asked.

"Mommy took them this morning," Shakira said.

"I don't know how she does it. I would be going crazy right now, especially with your three," Shante said, pointing at Shanice.

Shanice was so high that she just laughed at this.

"Light up another one. I need that right now," Shante said.

The girls sat in the living room, and Shanice and Shakira told Shante about their fight a few days earlier.

"Remember when daddy took us to the number house, and that guy owed him money?" Shanice said after their story.

"Yeah, I remember. He took a two-by-four with nails in it from the car and beat the guy's legs," Shakira said.

"I cried, and y'all just kept on playing in the car like it was nothing," Shante said.

"For some reason, he always took us along whenever he had to get back at somebody." Shakira said.

"Do you remember what he did to the paper deliveryman who smacked Mommy's ass?" Shanice said. They all laughed at the memory.

"I saw that man the other day. He is missing four fingers on his right hand," Shakira said.

"Daddy was a ruthless dude," Shante said.

"I think we all inherited that trait. I find myself doing crazy shit all the time," Shanice added. The girls laughed.

"I remember setting Trez's mattress on fire while he was on it 'cause he had slept with another girl there and refused to buy a new bed." The sisters laughed at this too.

"So what did he do?" Shante said.

"He bought a new bed after that. Shit, I was not playing," Shanice said, laughing. Shante loved chatting with her sisters, but when she got a text from Jared, she was ready to go see him.

"Has anybody talked to Shayla?" Shante said.

"Nah, she ain't even come to the hospital to see me," Shanice replied.

"Make sure y'all check the mailbox for your checks tomorrow," Shante said. She grabbed her purse and jacket. "I guess I will see y'all next week for Thanksgiving. I have a date tonight," Shante said.

"That young boy's putting it down, huh?" Shanice said.

"What are you talking about?" Shante said, laughing as she walked to the door.

"Yeah, let Brother Harry find out. What did he say the last time they argued, Shakira?" Shanice prompted.

"'I will kill you, bitch. Bet a fucking dollar on it,'" Shakira said, laughing.

"He was drunk as shit," Shanice said, also laughing.

"Well, what he doesn't know won't hurt him. Later, girls," Shante said. She fixed her hair and makeup when she got in the car. She got to Jared's apartment in less than fifteen minutes. It was in the Adams Run apartments, not far from where Shayla lived. He opened the door with no shirt on, and he was cooking for them.

"What's for dinner?" she asked.

"A little something. Take your coat off," he said, kissing her on the lips. She did what he suggested before she sat at the table and poured a glass of wine. He always bought her favorite, Red Moscato. He had a cute bachelor pad with brown microfiber furniture and wooden coffee tables. He lit candles on the dining room table and set silverware at their places. He brought her a plate full of shrimp Alfredo.

"How was your day?" he asked.

"It was good. I saw my sisters after work, and we talked and drank together."

"Really?" he said. "Can you stay the night?" he added, changing the subject.

"I want too, but I want it to be as peaceful as possible at home until I can afford to move away from him," she answered.

"I told you that I've got you if you'll just let me," he said.

"You are eighteen. I cannot possibly be a burden on you. Did you forget my kids? It's too much to ask so soon, but I do appreciate the offer," she said.

She made her way to his chair and sat on his lap.

"It won't be long, baby. You will see," she said.

"I want it to be right now. I am in love with you. I hate that you go home to him, and he talks to you all fucked up and treats you like shit, when I can love you better," he said emotionally.

"I hate that I came into your life and fucked it up," she said.

"No, you made it better," he said, kissing her on the lips. "I have something for you." He pushed her off of him gently, went to the closet, and pulled out a Gucci shopping bag.

"What's this?" she said.

"Open it," he replied.

She pulled out a black leather Gucci bag and a pair of knee-high boots to match.

"Wow, this must have cost you a lot," she said.

"Don't worry about that," he said.

He kissed her passionately and walked her toward his bedroom. He laid her on the bed and removing her clothes to expose her red thong and bra as he admired her body. He kissed her, starting with her lips and working his way to her erect nipples. She soon positioned herself on top of him, kissing his chest passionately and making her way to his love muscle. She devoured him until he was near explosion, and then she mounted herself on him and bounced until he exploded inside of her.

"Shante!" he yelled.

She fell asleep in his arms without a care in the world. She loved how he made her feel, and going home was the last thing she wanted to do. She got up around twelve thirty in the morning so that she could get home to the kids.

"You're leaving me?" he said, half-asleep.

"For now," she said, kissing him before she went. When Shante got home, Harold was sound asleep on the couch. The mail was on the table, and she could see the check from her father's estate. Her heart jumped, as she knew she could go straight to the realtor tomorrow. Her dream was finally a reality. With the $12,000 she had saved and the $10,000 in this check, she was going to leave Harold.

Chapter 9

Shayla

Shayla was called in to work on her day off. She usually didn't work on Fridays because the jail seemed so busy. She was working in the visiting room that day, and she hated seeing so many hopeless women visiting men who were playing them and would probably never change. She knew she was with one of these men too. Hick would never change, but she loved him so much. It was almost the end of her shift, and she was more than ready to leave. An officer brought her slips, and she called the front desk with the names of inmates to be sent in.

She called four names: Joseph Santos, Victor Franklin, Hakeem Jackson, and Hickson Johnson. Her heart dropped as she wondered who was visiting her man. She waited for the female visitors to walk up to be searched, hoping that Hick's mother was one of them. A Hispanic woman walked up, holding the slip with his name on it. She had a long weave, wore a black sweat suit, and looked a full nine months pregnant. Shayla was speechless. The woman's name was Samantha Rodriguez Johnson. "So he was married the whole time," Shayla thought. Her eyes welled up with tears as the relief for her shift came.

"What's up, girl?" Diamond said.

"That's what's up," she said, nodding toward Hick and his visitor.

"He is crazy. You got her name?" Diamond asked.

"Yup," Shayla replied.

"Pull up her info and pay her a visit," Diamond said.

"Ten steps ahead of you," Shayla said.

Shayla rushed out of the visiting room and went to the ladies room to wash her face. Diamond text-messaged her the woman's address and phone number. Shayla wondered how this had happened right under her nose. She regretted not checking his visitors. When she finally made it to her car, she felt nauseated and threw up on the side of her vehicle. "It's over," she thought. He had betrayed her again after everything she had risked to help him.

She went home to shower before she went to Samantha's house that night. Later, she threw on a pair of black tights, a gray Chanel sweater, a pair of black Chanel sneakers, and a black trench coat. Her hair was in a stylish pony tail. She pulled up the address on her GPS navigation system and found out that Samantha lived in Franklin Mills, about a thirty-minute-drive away. When Shayla pulled up, she was in awe. It was exactly what she wanted: a big house with a picket fence and two-car garage. The lawn was mowed perfectly. She walked up to the door and rang the bell.

Samantha answered the door and asked, "Can I help you?" She spoke properly, and Shayla realized her long hair didn't include extensions.

Shayla blurted out, "Are you married to Hick?"

"Who wants to know?" she asked.

"Me," Shayla replied.

"You're another one, huh?" Samantha's Spanish accent began to come out.

"Excuse me?" Shayla said, confused.

"Another one of the flunkies that run his drugs and money while he's in jail."

"I am no one's flunky. We have had a sexual relationship for two years."

Samantha laughed. "You and about five other girls." she said.

"Are y'all together or what?" Shayla asked.

"What the fuck do you think? We have been married five years, and he has never left me for a bitch he fucked," she said, pointing to her wedding ring.

"He's been with me on and off for two years. You just let your so-called man roam like that? Please," Shayla said.

"All dogs roam, looking for a bitch to bone. But they always find their way home," Samantha said.

"You said 'bitch' one too many times," Shayla said.

"You came to my house, questioning me about my husband while his kids are in the other room. You should have accepted your place and kept it. He is not going to be happy about this," Samantha said. She moved to walk back into the house, and Shayla walked toward her. Hick's wife pulled a silver .22 out from under her round stomach.

"Get the fuck out of here!" she yelled, pointing the gun at Shayla. She backed up toward her car as Samantha backed into the house and closed the door. Shayla ran to her car and then sat in total stupor. She vomited on the side walk. She loved Hick, but she hated that he had lied to her. The prepaid phone began to vibrate, and it wasn't him calling.

"Hello," she said.

"I have your keys. What time are you picking them up?" asked the voice on the other end. Shayla had almost forgotten about the business she was supposed to handle.

"Oh yeah, I almost called a locksmith," Shayla said. "Meet me at mommy's in an hour," the voice said.

She hung up and stepped on the gas to get there in time to pick up the drugs. She arrived in less than forty minutes. They met at the same place each time, an old warehouse. She pulled a small duffel bag out of the trunk of her black Range Rover. It held enough money for eight kilos of coke and ten pounds of exotic weed. She put her 45-caliber Smith and Wesson on her hip with one bullet in the chamber, just in case things didn't go as planned. A young, dark-skinned man came to the door of the warehouse.

"Hello, Mama. You got the money?" he asked. She passed the bag off to him as she walked in. He gave the bag to another guy, who took it in the back and counted the money. The first guy walked out with her stuff and put it in the trunk.

"Tell Hick it was nice doing business," he said, smiling. It was the same routine every time. Next, Shayla usually drove the product to Hick's friend who bagged and distributed. He gave her what she needed to put on the street and in the jail. Hick didn't trust his friends with his connect. Shayla had made that same run with him before he was arrested and now by herself since he had been locked up. Shayla decided she would not call his friends this time. Instead, she was going to put the entire run on the street herself. She threw her prepaid phone in the glove compartment and turned it off as she contemplated her next move. She knew how Hick was on the street and knew that his lawyer was expecting another $10,000 before the next hearing. Shayla had made up her mind after seeing his wife pregnant, when Shayla had already gotten two abortions because he said he wasn't ready for kids. She hated seeing her in the home she wanted. She wanted to be this man's wife, and he was using her as a drug mule. Shayla cried all night, thinking of the devastation he had caused her. She was going to get back at him. At one point, she called Diamond for more information. She picked up on the first ring.

"What's up, girl?" Diamond asked.

"What happened at the visit?" Shayla asked.

"Well, he rubbed her belly the whole time, and they laughed, joked, and kissed each other. I read their lips—you remember I learned how to because my brother is deaf? The baby is a girl, due any day now, and she's naming her Molly. He was worried about some personal business, and she kept telling him that it's taken care of. Nothing else, really—just a lot of kiss-face shit. He didn't know I was there until the visit was over, and then he almost shit himself when he saw me," Diamond said in almost one breath.

"He is in for a rude awaking. I'm taking all his shit and putting it on the streets myself," Shayla said.

"Really? Who's going to get rid of it?" Diamond asked.

"I was thinking about an enemy of his, Kyree, because I know he won't mind going at it with him when he comes home," Shayla said.

"What about Jermaine? I heard Kyree is crazy," Diamond said.

"What about him?" Shayla asked.

"He knows some people that might be interested," Diamond explained.

"There's not much he can do from jail, so tell him to get at me when he gets out," Shayla answered.

"Okay, so what about work? You know it's going to be crazy when he finds out," Diamond said.

"I guess I will take a leave of absence after all. I will call you tomorrow," Shayla said, hanging up.

Chapter 10

Thanksgiving

The turkey was in Ms. Sandy's oven, along with all the fixings. All the grandkids were there as well as a few other relatives. Ms. Sandy loved bringing all of her kids together. Her daughters helped prepare the food.

"Congrats on that game," Shayla said to Little Sterling. The family never missed any of his games, and he played well in all of them.

"You were out on that field today," Shanice added. Shayla walked upstairs to hide her emotions. As she cried alone in her mother's room, she received a call from Kyree. "He was Hick's right-hand man until they had a discrepancy about money, and Kyree's brother boo was dropped off at the ER and no one knew what happened. Kyree blamed Hick for this; he felt that Hick wanted the connect to himself. Kyree wasn't a snitch, and he was loyal to the streets. He was waiting for a moment to get back at Hick when he wasn't expecting it. Shayla knew that Kyree would love to put Hick's drugs on the streets. She contacted him, and they had talked back and forth ever since.

"I see you're getting rid of this shit fast," Shayla said.

"Yeah, Ma, you know how we do," He said.

"I am at a family gathering, so meet at the same place in the morning," she said.

"All right," he said, hanging up.

Shanice was high as a kite after popping four Xanax pills. The headaches were getting worse, but she never went to her follow-up appointment—the stitches fell out by themselves. She had found the guys who came into her house, and she spread the word about where Trez liked to hide out. She was waiting to get a call about them doing something to him.

Shante was in awe. She found a four-bedroom house in Montgomery County and expected to close on it in two weeks. She had decided that she would move out on Harold's birthday, two days after the closing date, and leave his divorce papers on the table.

Shakira had continued hustling weed, and she was ready to move on to something bigger. She wanted to ask Mika about the pill game but didn't want to step on her toes.

"Are you okay, Shanice?" Cassie asked Shanice, laughing with the friend she brought. Cassie was a cousin of theirs who always had something to say, and she would always hate on Shayla, Shante, Shanice, and Shakira because they stuck together.

"What's that supposed to mean?" Shakira said.

"She looks a little spaced," Cassie said.

"My sister just went through some shit that you will never be built to go through," Shakira said.

"You mean if I don't get my ass beat by my dude, I ain't been through anything?" Cassie said.

"No, I mean shut the fuck up before I bust your ass," Shakira replied. The house grew quiet as Shayla and Shante appeared. Shanice was completely out of it, sitting in the corner.

"What did you say?" Cassie said, standing up.

"You fucking heard me. Don't you ever come up in my mom's shit and talk shit about my sister in front of your bum-ass friends," Shakira said.

"You don't know me," Cassie's friend said.

"She ain't gotta know you," Shante retorted.

"Yeah, so get the fuck out before it's a serious problem," Shakira said. Ms. Sandy went into the kitchen. She hated when her girls were upset, and it was so hard to calm them down.

Silas came into the room and asked, "What's going on?"

"Nothing. Cassie and her friend were just leaving," Shante said.

"Word on the street is that all y'all marked for death. Die slow, bitches," Cassie said, walking out. Shakira had had enough of her mouth, so she went through the back door, followed by her sisters. Shakira ran around the side of the house and hit Cassie in the face as she came down the front steps. Cassie's friend tried to fight Shakira, but Shante punched her in the face, and she hit the ground. Shakira and Cassie began to fight, and they both fell on top of a car parked in front of the house. They both fell to the ground with Shakira on top. She punched Cassie in the face over and over, and Shayla jumped into the fight and kicked her in the head.

"Don't ever wish death on my family, bitch," Shakira said, spitting on Cassie. The rest of the family came outside as Cassie's mom—the girls' aunt—Bam, screamed.

"Get off my daughter!" she said. Ms. Sandy stood on the porch for a moment, shook her head, and went back into the house. Cassie had offended her girls, and she always told them that if they fought for anything, it should be respect. Everyone went back into the house for Thanksgiving dinner and left

Cassie and Bam outside. Cassie acted the way she did toward the girls because Aunt Bam secretly hated her sister, Ms. Sandy. Shayla, Shakira, and Shante took Shanice upstairs to bed, and she didn't argue. She was still completely out of it. The night ended late, so the girls stayed at their mother's house and slept in their old rooms. Ms. Sandy woke up the next morning and made her famous Thanksgiving omelet, adding turkey, stuffing, and sweet potatoes to the eggs. She made sweet potato oatmeal for her grandkids. It was like old times. Even Silas stayed there with his son.

"What happened last night?" Shanice asked.

"You got us into a fight even though you were high," Shante said.

"It was the damn pills," Shanice said.

"I think you took more than the prescribed dose," Silas said. They all laughed, knowing he was right. Ms. Sandy had been feeling down a lot recently, but this morning made her very happy.

"I want y'all here every Saturday for breakfast and every Sunday for dinner," she said.

"Sounds good to me," Shakira said, picking up her fork.

"I have an announcement. I am leaving Harold," Shante said with a big smile on her face.

"I found a place to buy in Montgomery County for the kids and me, and I am divorcing him," Shante said. Tears rolled down her face when she noticed her family's shock.

"I haven't told him or the kids yet, but I needed to share it with someone," she said. Everyone looked at her.

"What happened?" Ms. Sandy asked.

"He happened—the cheating, the verbal abuse. I hate him more than I can imagine. Every day, I wonder how I can kill him and get away with it," Shante confessed.

"You know that we would have helped you with that, Sis," Shanice said.

"I know, but the kids . . ." Shante said, cracking a smile.

"You're just going to leave that man? He has a good job, and he loves his kids," Ms. Sandy said, taking Harold's side.

"Mom, he doesn't love me, and it shows. That's all that matters," Shante said.

"He has supported you all this time. What are you going to do for money?" Ms. Sandy said.

"I work, Mom, and make good money. I will be teaching a class in January by myself," Shante said.

"If you say so," Ms. Sandy replied.

"It's as if you have no faith in me," Shante said.

"He works for the city," Ms. Sandy reminded her.

"Why does a black man only have to get a decent job before he thinks he can do whatever he wants and treat his woman the way he wants," Shante said. All her sisters agreed.

"I love my father, but he cheated on you, Mom, and sometimes he talked to you fucked up. You never fought for his respect, but you would always beat a bitch down for chasing after him, all because he had a good job and paid the bills. You taught me to fight for respect, and I am. No man with a good job is excused. I am leaving Harold, and that's that," Shante said.

"You're leaving daddy?" said her eight-year-old, Morgan. Shante looked at her daughter in shock because she wasn't ready to discuss it with her.

"Yes, baby," Shante said.

"You don't love daddy anymore?" she asked.

"No, I don't, and he doesn't love me," she said.

"So no more fighting and him calling you names?" Morgan asked.

"No, we'll have a new home, and you can see your father whenever you want. I would never take that from you," Shante said.

"Okay, I understand," said her daughter.

"If you have any questions, just come to me," Shante said, kissing her daughter on the forehead. Ms. Sandy looked hurt as she heard what her granddaughter was going through. Shante's sisters, who had envied her, saw marriage in a new light.

"I wish I would have known, Sis. I would have fucked him up," Silas said.

Knock, knock, knock!

"Who is it?" Ms. Sandy said, walking to the door as she tried not to cry.

"We have a warrant for Shakira and Shanice Savage," said the voice at the door.

"Shit, that bitch pressed charges," Shanice said.

"Remember, y'all don't know shit. I will bail you out," Ms. Sandy said. The girls had been locked up plenty of times, and they knew what fighting the cops would get them.

The kids were in the dining room eating their oatmeal, so Shante took them upstairs while the cops took Shakira and Shanice away quickly. "You could start a daycare with all their kids," Silas said.

"Shut up, Silas!" Shante said. They all laughed at his joke. As the kids came back downstairs, Dallas said, "Where my mom?"

"She will be back," Shayla said.

"She in jail again, with my mom," Corrie said. The kids went on with their day, never shedding a tear. They were used to their moms getting locked up.

Chapter 11

Shakira

Shakira had spent the whole weekend in jail. They released her and Shanice after Shayla paid their bail. When Shakira walked into the house, the TV was on, and she heard some noise upstairs. She instantly knew it was Steven, and she forgot he had a key to her house.

"Steven!" she yelled as she slammed the door. "What the fuck are you doing here?"

"So it's like that?" he said.

"I see you're in pocket with the weed and juice and shit. I got rid of some of that for you in case you needed lawyer money," he said.

"Who the fuck told you to touch my shit?" she asked. She pulled open her closet and saw that most of her purple was gone.

"Where the fuck is my money, Steven?" she asked, holding her hand out. He slammed a bundle of bills into her hand that added up to $1,000. She looked through the tote where she kept everything, and only four pints of purple remained from a whole case. She knew she had spent almost $4,000 on product.

"I took my cut off the top," he said.

"What the fuck did you buy? How you gonna come in my house and take my shit and my money?" Shakira cried as her heart raced faster. She thought about everything she wanted to do for herself and her kids. She sat on the bed as Steven just stood by the door, smoking a blunt nonchalantly. His phone began to ring, and Shakira heard a girl's voice on the other end when he answered.

"I am at my baby mom's house," he said. The voice on the other end replied as he said, "Nah, this is just business. I will call you later so we can hook up." Shakira slapped the phone out of his hand and punched him in the face. He grabbed her by the face, pushed her onto the bed, and climbed on top of her.

"You mad, huh? You mad? Calm the fuck down," he whispered in her ear. He licked her face as she kept fighting him.

"Get the fuck off of me!" she yelled.

"You want me to fuck you?" He pulled her pants down, pulled his erect love muscle out, and slid inside of her. She stopped fighting and allowed him to stroke her. He exploded within minutes.

"That's all your worth—pussy," he said.

"Get off of me," she said, wiping herself off with a towel.

He spit in her face as he got up. Shakira jumped up and attacked him again, but he threw her to the floor. She felt around for the metal bat under her bed, picked it up, and jumped up. As Steven turned around to walk away, she hit the back of his head, and he hit the floor. She stood over him and hit him in the head again and again. Blood splattered all over the walls and the bed. Her body was covered with blood, and his face was disfigured. He gasped for air through the blood running down his throat.

"I fucking hate you. Get the fuck up! Get up," she yelled and pulled on him. He lay there, and she watched him convulse. She looked at him with hatred. She remembered all the times she cried over him and how many girls he cheated on her with.

All she had ever wanted was for him to love her. Instead, he had taken everything from her. He didn't even care about their daughter. She couldn't think of the last time he had held her. She grabbed a pillow, placed it over his face, and suffocated him. He didn't fight at all. When she removed the pillow, he had stopped breathing and his eyes had rolled toward the back of his head.

Shakira ran to the bathroom and grabbed rubber gloves from under the sink. She dug in his pockets and found the money he had taken. She ran down to the basement and grabbed tape, thick plastic sheeting, a bucket, and bleach. When she went back upstairs, she noticed that her sectional rug was heavy with the blood it had soaked up. She laid the plastic across the floor and pulled his lifeless body onto it. She wrapped his plastic-covered body extra tightly with the tape. Then she took up the rug and put it in a trash bag. She took all her clothes off and put them in a separate bag with the sheets from the bed and the rags and towels she used to wipe off the walls. She grabbed one of his cigarettes and smoked it as she watched him for hours, waiting for night to fall.

Shanice called her, and she knew Shanice would help get rid of the body. But Shanice was already in trouble. Shakira needed someone tall to come to the house and drive the body away in his truck somewhere, and the only person she could think of was Silas. He didn't listen, and he always managed to fuck something up, so he was her last resort. Silas was a broke hustler who would pull a trigger without killing anyone.

"Silas, I need you, now," Shakira said when she called him.

"What's wrong?"

"It's a family thing," she said.

"You want me to call Shanice and everyone?" he asked.

"No, just you," she said. Silas got there fast since he was around the corner at Ms. Sandy's house. When he walked in, she threw him plastic gloves.

"Aw shit, what the fuck happened? You just got out of jail this morning," he said.

"The less you know, the better," she replied. He followed her to the bedroom, and he saw the body wrapped in plastic on the floor.

"What, did he hit you or something?" he said.

"I met him," she said.

"This is fucking Steven? You got a change of clothes for me?" he asked.

"You don't need new clothes. Just leave all your belongings—even your phone. I wrapped him up real good," she said. They pulled the body downstairs and turned out all the lights in the house. It was one in the morning and really cold, so no one was outside.

They grabbed the trash bags and the body and put everything in the back of Steven's truck. Before they left, they tied a cinder block from the basement to his feet. The plan was to dispose of the body in the Schuylkill River, but they drove around for an hour, and there was always someone lurking around.

"What the fuck? Why is everyone outside all of a sudden?" Shakira said, getting frustrated.

"Yeah, I am starting to get tired," Silas said.

"Fuck it. We can dump this shit in Camden. I know a little bridge. It's dark, and no one will be out there. Plus, he claimed to be hustling over there," Shakira said.

They pulled their hoods up as they crossed the bridge in case any cameras caught them, and Shakira hid in the backseat. They parked the truck on the end of a small bridge on State Street in Camden. They took the body out of the truck and struggled to carry it to the bridge. It was pitch black and deserted, just as Shakira expected.

"Good, the water is high," Shakira said, looking over the bridge. They both crawled down as they rolled the body halfway down the hill leading to the water.

"I don't believe this shit," Shakira said.

"What, that you killed your baby daddy," Silas asked.

"Not that. I am sliding in fucking mud," she said. They finally got close enough to roll the body into the water. He floated, so they waited for him to go under water

"What the fuck! Why is this taking so long?" Silas asked.

"I don't know. He won't stop floating," Shakira said.

"Look, we gotta go before we get caught," Silas said.

"What if he doesn't sink?" she asked. She approached his body and noticed that the cinder block had not gone under. She pushed it in, and he finally began to sink. They climbed back up the hill and quickly ran back to Steven's car.

"Where we gonna dump this car?" Silas asked.

"Back in Philly, so they won't think to look for him here," Shakira suggested.

"Sis, I will get rid of the truck. Go to Mom's and get some sleep. You look like you've been through a lot," he said.

"Get rid of the truck, Silas—no bullshit," she said. Silas dropped Shakira off at Ms. Sandy's house. She jumped in the shower and then burned her clothes and shoes, the rug, and the sheets in the grill. She put the remains in a trash can outside to be picked up in the morning. Shakira called Steven's cell phone and left a few messages, just in case someone looked through phone records. She felt a sense of relief, like she had finally gotten over Steven. She knew he would never be with anyone else. He couldn't treat her like shit anymore or throw other females in her face. It was finally over. She hugged her kids tight as she cuddled with them in the full-sized bed in the room that was hers when she was younger. The baby was sleeping with Ms. Sandy who was sound asleep in her room with the door closed. Shakira slept until about nine thirty in the morning and then called Steven's mom before she beat her to it.

"Hello," said his mom.

"Have you seen Steven?" Shakira asked.

"No, he told me he had to make some moves," his mom answered.

"He told me the same thing last night, but he never came back to my house," Shakira said.

"Let me call him. He usually either calls or comes home," his mom said.

"Well, if you talk to him before I do, tell him to call me, because I need to take Gazelle to the ER. She has an ear infection," Shakira said.

"Okay, I will tell him," his mom said. Shakira went back to sleep with only two thoughts on her mind: She was going to get back the money that he fucked up, and she was going to clean her room again to make sure she removed all of the blood.

Chapter 12

Shanice

Shanice came home to an empty house, and her head was pounding so hard that she could barely see. She lay down and tried to recover her vision. She called a friend who lived around the corner, Janae, for help. She came right over and helped Shanice take medicine for the headache. Shanice finally felt some relief after another hour. Janae stayed and watched her sleep, hoping she was okay. Janae loved her more than Shanice would ever know. Shanice never got too close to Janae because she thought her friend being a lesbian was contagious. She woke up to Janae watching TV on the other couch and talking on the phone.

"Thank you for coming," Shanice said.

"You're welcome," Janae said as she told the person on the phone that she would call them back.

"I would have called my sisters, but I knew you were closer," Shanice said.

"It's okay. Are you all right?" Janae asked. "I hate to burden you with madness, but Stacy and Trez are still messing around. Word on the street is, she's pregnant by him and they've been messing around for a while," Janae said.

Shanice's head instantly hurt all over again. She went into the bathroom with her cell phone and called Tank, her friend who was cousins with the boys who tried to stick her up. He didn't answer, so she texted him: "I know that Trez is at Stacy's house every night. How have they not found him yet?" She hoped that he would call her right back. She hated everything that she was going through because of Trez, and it seemed that he was untouchable.

"Are you okay?" Janae asked, knocking on the bathroom door.

"Yeah, I am," Shanice said, coming from the bathroom.

"I think I am going to stay at my mom's house for a few days, until I can take care of myself. Can you drop me off?" Shanice asked.

"Yeah, I can take you. Let me get my car and check on my mom. I will be right back," Janae said.

While Janae was gone, Shanice took a long, hot shower and got dressed in a black sweat suit. She put her coat and hat on and filled a duffel bag with clothes for her and the boys, who were already at Ms. Sandy's. While she slept on the couch and waited for Janae to come back, she got a call from Trez. "Hello," she said.

"I want to see my fucking sons," he demanded.

"No, you don't. You just want to make my life hell. You're still fucking Stacy, and that bitch got me booked," she said.

"Do you know how many stitches she had to get in her pussy? Whoever kicked her between her legs fucked her up," he replied.

"Whatever. That sure ain't keeping you from fucking her," Shanice said.

"She sucked my dick," Trez said, laughing.

"Did you find the dudes who pistol-whipped me?" Shanice asked.

"I ain't worried about them niggas. They know where I am," he said.

"So no revenge for me, huh?" Shanice said.

"You're tough. You will be all right. When they come, I will take care of them," he said.

"Okay, I will talk to you later. I am going out now. When I get back, I will call so you can see the boys," she said. Shanice cried her heart out as she waited for Janae to pick her up. She wanted Trez to die, and she didn't have the strength to do it herself. She hoped Tank would call her, so she kept looking at her phone. Janae came back to pick her up, and when she got to Ms. Sandy's, Shakira was there. Their mother was frying chicken and making potato salad. All the kids stayed home from school that Monday and Tuesday because of the events that took place over the weekend. Shaniece couldn't wait to talk to her sister about what was happening. Shakira was lying on the couch with the baby.

"Sis, wake up. What's going on?" Shanice asked.

"I came here this morning," Shakira said.

"You know Trez is still fucking Stacy," Shanice said.

"What?" Shakira said.

"I don't know what to do. The dudes that were at my house haven't hit him up yet. I am so curious why. I haven't been in the streets in a couple days, so I need to hit a few bars and see what's going on. I told them where he lives and everything. It's been almost two weeks since it happened," Shanice said, frustrated.

"Who were the guys?" Shakira said.

"The Hawks brothers," Shanice said.

"They don't work like that. Who told you it was them?" Shakira asked.

"Stacey said they wanted Trez because he took money from them," Shanice explained.

"The Hawks brothers would have killed everybody in the house and then gone looking for Trez," Shakira said.

"I can't remember that night at all. Stacey said she answered the door and they grabbed me and pistol-whipped me," Shanice said.

Shanice's phone rang.

"Hello," she said.

"This is Tank. Sis, what are talking about? After you called me last week, I asked my boys if they knew anything about that, and that's a negative," Tank said.

"I'm trying to figure out why Stacy would tell my man that it was your boys," Shanice said.

"It was some young boys in the neighborhood, Sticks, Raz, and Jim," Tank said.

"Did you say 'Jim'?" Shanice confirmed.

"Yeah, he lives right around your way," he said.

"Yeah, I fucking know. That's Stacey's brother," Shanice said.

"Get the fuck out of here. So your girl set you up?" Tank asked.

"This is some bullshit. For fucking what? I know it wasn't to get at Trez. Did she think I had some money?" Shanice said.

"I heard she's fucking Trez now. Shit, she might get that nigga hit up soon," Tank said.

"Not if I kill her first for what she did to me. Did you hear what he did? He acted like he ain't care about who pistol-whipped me," Shanice said.

"Yeah, I was tripping when everybody said somebody was looking for him. But he was in the street like it wasn't about nothing. It ain't my niggas though. My niggas go hard," Tank replied.

"I will talk to you later," she said. They both hung up, and Shanice started to dial Trez's number, but then she stopped.

"Never mind. He doesn't know that I know Stacey set me up," Shanice said.

"Why did she set you up?" Shakira said.

"I don't know. Is she so fucking jealous of me that she wants to see me dead? That doesn't sound right," Shanice said.

"I am gonna need a night out to holler at a few people to see what's going on," Shanice said. Shanice got dressed to go out with Shakira. She wore a pair of black leggings, a black sweater that came to her hips and hung over her shoulders, a leather jacket, and a pair of black knee-high boots with a small heel. She threw on a long wig since she still had a bald spot on her head. Shakira wore a pair of dark-denim jeans, a fitted black shirt, a pair of black boots, and a leather jacket just like Shanice's. Shakira straightened her hair with a flat iron and picked up her small MK tote to hold her fully loaded .22 caliber. They left their mother's house at ten at night, after putting the kids to sleep. They went to a neighborhood bar called Dices, where most of the people from Shanice's neighborhood hung out. When they got inside, a friend of Trez's named Boodu walked up.

"I thought you were dead," he said.

"That shit ain't fucking funny," Shanice said.

"My bad, boo. You good though," Boodu said, hugging her.

"Yo, I thought you was gonna kill Stacey when you found out the shit that she pulled. That was smart to just beat the shit out of her. Everybody knew what she did, so if she had gone missing, they would have looked at y'all. I know the shit y'all are into," Boodu said.

"You don't know shit," Shanice said, walking to the bar and sitting down to order a drink.

"Hey, Dimples," Shanice said to the bartender.

"What the fuck is up, girl? I heard that sucker shit Stacey did," Dimples said.

"What did you hear?" Shanice asked.

"I heard she sent Jim and his young boys to rob you, something about you getting ten thousand dollars from your pop dying. She thought you cashed the check and had the money in the house," Dimples said.

"That's crazy. I never cashed the check," Shanice said. She had deposited it in her account instead of cashing it.

"I also heard you dug into her ass literally, and she and Trez had been fucking on the regular, even before this happened. That's my girl," Dimples said, giving Shanice a high five. "What y'all drinking? It's on me."

"We'll both have Grey Goose and cranberry," Shanice said.

"I don't believe this shit. Did you tell her about the money?" Shakira asked.

"Yeah, and I know it's true, 'cause she's the only one I told," Shanice said.

"What you want to do?" Shakira asked.

"I want to kill this bitch slowly," Shanice replied.

"You know I got you, Sis. It's whatever," Shakira said.

Chapter 13

Shante

Shante was in awe after closing on her new house. She called Jared because she knew he would be happy for her.

"Who's this?" a girl on the other end said, answering the call.

"Where's Jared?" Shante asked.

"He's a little busy right now. I will have him call you back." The girl hung up.

Shante's heart shattered. She was beyond hurt. But then she laughed at herself. "I fell in love with a little boy. What did I expect?" she asked herself.

She was too happy to let that bring her down. She was ready to close the Harold chapter in her life. Her phone began to ring, and it was Jared's number. She ignored his call and turned off the ringer. She drove home with the biggest smile on her face, feeling like she had just conquered the world. When she arrived home, it was nice outside for December. Harold was in the kitchen, talking to one of his girlfriends on the phone.

"Can I talk to you for a minute?" Shante asked.

"What is it?" he replied.

"I want to give you what you want," Shante said.

"Let me call you back," Harold said into the phone and then hung up.

"You leaving?" he said.

"I am going to stay with my mom for a while," Shante said, lying.

"What about my kids?" he asked.

"You are free to see the kids whenever you like," she said.

"What about support for the kids?" Harold said.

"You can do what you've been doing. That's fine with me," she answered.

"So when are you leaving?" he asked.

"Today." Harold's face turned from looking stony to hurt.

"Why the sad face? I thought you wanted me gone," Shante said.

"I want you gone, not my kids," he said as he threw his coffee in her face.

Shante screamed. It surprised and scared her, but the coffee wasn't hot enough to burn her. He walked up the steps, and she followed.

"This is how we solve this—by throwing tantrums? They are my kids too. I would never just leave them. You work more than me, so I thought it would only be right for me to have them most of the time," she explained.

"I'm at the end of my rope with you," he said, going into his closet.

Shante just wanted closure, and she thought it would make him happy if they went their separate ways.

"I want to be happy, Harry. It's obvious that I don't make you happy, and you don't make me happy either," Shante said.

He pulled out some clothes and changed to go out.

"Just do what you have to do. As long as I can see my kids, I am fine," he said.

Shante knew that wasn't the end of it. He wasn't sarcastic or gloating, which told her she had really hurt him. She almost felt sorry for him.

Her phone vibrated as a text from Jared came in.

"I am so sorry. My baby's mom got hold of my phone. I picked my daughter up to take her to see my mom. I would never do anything to hurt you. Please answer your phone," Jared wrote.

Jared never really talked about his daughter because it was such a struggle with her mother. Shante instantly called him.

"I got the house," she said.

"You did? Baby, I am so happy for you. You tell him you leaving yet?" Jared asked.

"Yeah," she whispered.

"What the fuck did he do?" Jared said.

"He was sad about it, and I am scared. I don't know his next move, but I know I need to get out of here as soon as possible," she said. Harold walked downstairs and out the front door in silence as Shante continued her conversation.

"Where are the kids?" Jared asked.

"They are packing their stuff. Can you come over tonight when the kids are asleep?" Shante asked.

"Yes, I will be there. I love you, Shante," he said.

"I love you too. I will text you the new address," she said. She put her phone down, packed her belongings, and piled as much as she could in the truck. She made five trips and was extremely tired by the time she was done. She left all the furniture and TVs. It took hours to get situated in the new house. She laid the kids down in their new beds, the only furniture she was able to purchase. Soon, she heard her phone ring.

"Are the kids sleeping?" Jared asked.

"Yeah," she said.

"Open the door for me. I'm cold," he said.

She opened the door in a towel, as she was just getting out of the shower when he called. He walked in and kissed her, removing her towel and laying her on the carpeted floor.

"You are so beautiful," he said as he looked into her eyes. The phone rang. The call was from a blocked number, so she decided not to answer and ruin the moment. She had never felt so free while she was with him.

The next morning, a Saturday, Shante woke Jared up before the kids got up.

"I hate to leave you," he said.

"I hate to let you go. I feel like we are still sneaking around," she said.

"I understand you not wanting me around the kids just yet. They need time to heal. And I love you, so I know I will love them." He threw on his basketball pants and hoodie. He kissed her passionately and snuck out of the room. Shante felt really good. A little while later, the kids ran to her room, asking for breakfast. Shante made pancakes in her new kitchen. She looked around the house, admiring the patio doors and big windows looking into her yard, the marble countertops and marble floors in the kitchen, the plush carpet, and the smell of fresh paint. She put a down payment on her own house with her own money, when Harold said she couldn't. Her daydreams came to a halt when she heard a knock at the door. She ran, thinking it was Jared. But her smile turned into a frown when she saw Harold there, holding some papers.

"You shouldn't leave paperwork around." He pushed his way in. "You told me you were moving to your mom's! You bought a house in the suburbs," he said with sarcasm.

"Yes, and it's mine, and you are not welcome here," she said.

"Daddy!" Megan yelled. All the kids ran to see him.

"Are you moving with us?" Mathew asked.

"Yeah, Daddy will be here with y'all soon. I just have to make it up to your mom," he said.

"It's too late for that. Now that you know where I live, don't come over here uninvited. You know that Montgomery County police don't play with domestic abuse charges," Shante said.

"I won't. I wouldn't want to scare your little boyfriend," he said.

"Get out!" she said. Harold walked out, looking at her with wild eyes.

"This is not the end of this conversation," he said.

"There is no more to talk about. I am through with being your doormat," she said.

"We are not divorced! I am not through with you yet!" he yelled. He calmed down as the kids ran to the door to say good-bye.

"You will see," he said.

Shante slammed the door in his face. She called Jared, and he answered on the first ring.

"What's up?" he asked.

"Harold knows where I live, and he just threatened me. I don't know what to do," she said.

"Don't worry, babe. I will be right there," Jared said. Shante sent the kids to their rooms and paced the floor as she waited for Jared. He walked right in and hugged her.

"I have something for you," he said. He gave her a .22-caliber gun that looked like it had just been polished. She took it and pointed it at the door. "I will show you how to shoot it," he offered.

"No need. I frequent the gun range. I just never bought a gun, because I never thought I would have to use it," Shante said.

"I know that if I lost a good woman like you, I would come and fight for you," Jared said. His phone rang, and he took the call. Shante kept admiring the gun as he talked on the phone.

"I have to make a run. I will be right back," he said. He kissed her passionately. "Where are you going?" she asked.

"On a little run," he said.

"What time will you be back?" she asked.

"In a few," he answered, smacking her ass playfully. Shante loved the affection she got from him. It was more than she had gotten from her husband. She didn't know what to expect from Harold, but she knew that he was ruthless and she had to put up her guard.

Chapter 14

Shayla

It had been three weeks since Shayla last spoke to Hick. He called every day, wanting to talk to her, and she didn't answer. She wondered if his wife had told him that she spoke to her, and she hated the fact that she never got a chance to tell him how she felt. Shayla decided that today, when he called, she would speak her mind. The package was gone, and she was more than ready to re-up, but she was scared to go alone. She sat in the house and counted money all day. She had made it all back and then some. She realized that the $10,000 he gave her each run was bullshit. Her phone rang, and she picked it up quickly.

"What's up, sweetness?" Kyree said.

"Nothing, nigga. Where the rest of my money?" she said.

"It's coming," he said. Shayla didn't trust him. In the last two weeks, he had managed to kill four people. However, she knew Kyree was ruthless, and she needed that to move the product.

"I'm just seeing what's up with you and if everything is okay," he said.

"Everything is fine. Why are you so concerned?" she asked.

"You allowed a nigga to eat when he was starving. I gotta make sure the boss is okay," he replied.

"Well, I wouldn't call me that just yet. I need to make another run, and the boss is kind of shaken," she said.

"What does that mean?" he asked.

"I know you know what to expect. I took that shit from Hick," she said.

"You robbed his connect?" he asked.

"No, I paid for it with his money and took the whole supply. I haven't talked to him since. When I linked up with you, I was in a bind because I didn't know how to get rid of that type of work," she said.

"If you need muscle, you got it. That was kinda gangsta," he said.

"I'm waiting on the call to let me know what time to pick it up," she said.

"You don't have to go alone—I've got your back. Call me if you need me," he said, hanging up. She had gone on her own for the last few weeks, and she didn't know if Hick had reached out. So she waited patiently for Hick and the connect to call as she counted the money and placed it in her black duffel bag. She didn't want Kyree to find out who the connect was. Hick had taught her to never share one. Shayla decided to take a chance with tonight's run. If they knew anything was up, they wouldn't call her. She shopped for clothes online as she drank a glass of wine. Her leave of absence, claiming she needed to take care of her ill mother, was approved. She grew nauseated, and as she felt vomit in the back of her mouth, she ran to bathroom. She threw up the wine and half of her lunch. In the past, she had only ever thrown up when she was pregnant. She cried, hoping that it wasn't the reason this time. It would be her fourth pregnancy in two years. Shayla had gotten two abortions, and then she miscarried the last fetus. She looked in the bathroom cabinets for a pregnancy test right away. She found one under the sink and quickly peed in a small disposable cup. She dipped the stick in the cup and waited for what seemed like a lifetime. The result was positive. She vomited more as she started crying. She knew that she couldn't just ignore Hick in jail. She hated to either get another abortion or have his baby. Soon, the prepaid phone rang with a call from a blocked number.

"You left your keys at my house," the voice said.

"Oh really? What time can I pick them up?" she asked.

"I should be home around eight tonight," he said. "Make sure you bring me twenty of your mom's cookies," he said. This meant that the pickup was at eight, and she needed $200,000 to get everything. It was always the same order every time. It was obvious that Hick didn't trust any of his workers. He only allowed Shayla access because he felt she wouldn't cross him. Shayla threw out the pregnancy test and got dressed. She threw on a pair black sweat pants, a black pullover hoodie, and an all-black pair of Air Max shoes. She put on her leg holster and placed her .22-millimeter in it. Shayla had never gone to meet the connect armed, but this time she felt like something was going to happen. When she reached the end of the block, she noticed a white Range Rover following her. She immediately looked in the rearview mirror and noticed it was Hick's wife. Shayla sped through the light, made a right-hand turn on a small street, and pulled over. The Range Rover pulled up behind her. She jumped out of the car with her gun in hand as she approached the car. Hick's wife jumped out of her car.

"What the fuck are you trying to do, stealing from Hick?" Samantha said in her Spanish accent.

"I didn't steal a thing. I took what belongs to me for all my pain and suffering," Shayla said, still holding the gun discreetly.

"Hick said to keep the money, but he wants the connect back. Give me the phone," she demanded.

"Tell Hick to kiss my ass. The connect is mine," Shayla said.

"You're stealing from a bunch of hungry, thirsty niggas that will kill you. I don't think you're ready for that," Samantha said, reaching for her back. Shayla pulled her gun out and pointed it at Hick's wife.

"Don't move! The next time you talk to Hick, tell him to go to hell. I suggest that you don't confront me again, or else you're going to have a problem. Now, get in your car and drive off," Shayla said. Samantha backed up toward her car as Shayla held the gun on her.

She pulled off fast and yelled, "You're a dead woman!"

"Congratulations!" Shayla said, noticing that Samantha wasn't pregnant anymore. Shayla looked at her license plate, which read, "SAAM4." She remembered it so that she could find more info on the woman. Shayla jumped back into her car and sped off to her destination. It took almost forty minutes to get to the warehouse. Shayla pulled up and grabbed the duffel bag as she got out of the car. She walked slowly to the door of the warehouse and knocked. The same guy who was usually there opened the door.

"Fish wants to talk to you," he said.

"Who?" Shayla asked. Everyone in the room laughed.

"The boss," he said. He started down a long hall and added, "Follow me."

The hall led to an office furnished with a large wooden desk and a leather office chair that faced the window.

"You are Shayla?" Fish asked in a deep voice.

"Yes," she said.

"What happened to Hick?" he said.

"He's in jail," she said.

"I've watched you come here for the last few weeks. You can't possibly handle all that work on your own. Are you still connected to him from jail?" Fish asked.

"We parted ways recently," she said.

"I do business with you and only you now," he announced.

"That's fine with me," she said.

"Hick is messy. I like quiet money. Don't bring bullshit into my business, and we can be great partners," he said.

"Whatever happened to Boo?" he asked.

"He was killed a few months ago," she said.

"You can leave the money. Your product is in the front. I will be in touch in three weeks with a direct number to me in case you have any trouble. Did you ever hear, 'More money, more problems'? It will start soon, and you will need muscle. Just don't cross me."

Shayla was relieved that she had established a relationship with the connect. The whole time they talked, he never turned around to show her his face.

Shayla walked to the front as the guys put the product in her trunk. She sped off, called Kyree, and asked him to meet her at Chili's for drinks. She didn't want him to know where she lived. He jumped out of his black Chevy Impala, wearing a red Phillies baseball jacket, fitted hat, dark-denim jeans, and a fresh pair of tan Timberland boots. His brown skin glowed, and the old scar that ran from his right ear to his chin added a roughness to him. As he approached the bar, Shayla felt herself heating up.

"You clean up well," she said as he walked toward her.

"How are you?" he said. When he hugged her, she felt the gun on each hip and the bulletproof vest he wore.

"You look cute in your dressed-down mode," he said after the waiter seated them.

"Whatever. I asked you to come out here because I am trying to make moves. Can I trust you?" she asked.

"You can, baby girl, but don't give me too much too soon. I like the mysterious you," he said.

She laughed.

"Now that that's settled, I am going to set up shop in one of my rental properties. I will let you know the address. The package is in, so your boys need to get to work," she said.

"Check you out, boss lady. You have your own package out," he said, laughing.

"Well, I need purple bags—we're going to call it 'lavender love,'" She said. They laughed and talked, enjoying each other's company. When they finished their meal, they walked out together. He walked her to her car, hugged her good-bye, and kissed her cheek. The smell of his cologne drew her in.

"Follow me home. I need my muscle with me," she said. He agreed. After she pulled her car into the garage, she ran to the front door to let him in. He walked in, embracing her and kissing her right on the lips. She kissed him back, and then she pushed him away.

"Just stay with me," she said. Shayla led him to her room, and they both slept in her bed. He held her most of the night. She didn't know if she could completely trust him, but she felt safe for the moment. The sun was bright as she woke up to the sound of her doorbell ringing. When she opened the door, she found a basketball sitting in red paint. The attached letter said, "It's about to get personal." Shakira yelled for Kyree, and he ran downstairs.

"What does this mean?" she asked him.

"This is Hick's bullshit," he explained.

"I know it's getting a little deep, but I can't take someone dying over this shit," she said.

"Don't worry. I've got you," Kyree said.

"No, fuck this." She called Hick on the phone she smuggled in the jail for him.

"Hello," he said.

"What does this mean?" she asked.

"What?" he said.

"The fucking basketball!" she answered.

"You will see," he said before he hung up.

"Let me call Diamond," Shayla said.

Diamond answered on the first ring.

"What's up?" Diamond said.

"Do you know who has been visiting Hick?" Shayla asked.

"It's been a bunch of Hispanics and his mom lately. But I haven't been in the visiting room, so I couldn't read his lips," Diamond said.

"It's getting crazy. When you get a chance, come and see me," Shayla said.

"I wanted to get with you anyway, because Jermaine is home and he wanted to get that package," Diamond said.

"How much?" Shayla asked.

"A whole chumpie," Diamond replied.

"That's thirty eight thousand. Just call me when he's ready," Shayla said. Shayla knew that Jermaine didn't have the money, and Diamond would do anything to be with him. Now she would have to watch her friend closely.

*   *   *

Diamond

"She said thirty-eight," Diamond said, nudging Jermaine as he slept in her bed.

"What?" he said.

"How much did you think it would be? I don't have that type of money," Diamond said.

"I'm going to have to get something smaller. Let me call my man, Trez," he said.

"Whatever," Diamond said as she got up to get dressed. She hated dealing with drugs. She had lost her brother because of them, so the less she knew, the better off she would be.

Chapter 15

Shakira

It had been a long couple of weeks, and Shakira was beyond tired of faking her concern for Steven. New Year's Eve was coming up, and Shakira did not want to spend it pretending to mourn. Steven's mother finally had a candlelight vigil, followed by dinner, in hopes they would find him. She felt depressed and a little resentful for what she had done. Steven's mother wanted to be closer to Shakira and the baby, and Shakira just wanted to part ways with it all. She dressed Gazelle for the vigil event and took the other kids to her mom's house. She didn't want to put them through that since Steven wasn't their father. Shakira had recently bought a black Buick Lucerne 2010. She had managed to get some ecstasy pills and oxycodone, and the college kids loved her. She didn't tell Mika because she knew her friend would be mad. They had been friends since kindergarten, but Shakira's love for her children was greater than her loyalty to Mika. She got dressed in a black suit and wore her hair straight. She knew that all of Steven's other baby moms would be there as well as the girl who had called her phone. His mom rented a big hall and asked a few people to speak on his behalf. She displayed a lot of pictures of him and the kids, and she even showed a home movie with clips of Steven. Shakira started to fall asleep as she listened to the preacher, but she wore dark shades so that no one could see her eyes. Shanice had gone with her for support, and she held the baby, rubbed Shakira's back, and told her it would be all right. Shanice didn't know that Shakira had something to do with Steven's disappearance. She never had a chance to tell her. The service was finally over, so Shakira dressed the baby in her little jacket and got ready to leave.

"You're not staying?" Shanice asked.

"No, I am ready to go," she said. Shanice grabbed her jacket, and the sisters passed all the other leaving guests.

"Hey, Shakira!" a voice yelled. Shakira turned around. It was Steven's latest girlfriend, Summer. Shakira stopped in Summer's path.

"You don't fucking know me to be calling me like that," Shakira said.

"I know that you know who did this to Steven. You didn't want to see us together, and it killed you that I am having his baby," she said, crying.

"Are you fucking crazy? No matter how many of you hos he gets pregnant, he always comes back to me. If you ever say that shit again, I will break your fucking jaw, pregnant and all. So watch your fucking mouth," Shakira yelled.

One of Summer's friends walked over to get her, and she cried as she walked away. Shakira left with Shanice and the baby. When they got in the car, it was silent for a moment.

"You did it, didn't you?" Shanice asked.

"Yeah, and I felt good about it until I came here. Now I feel guilty. I've never felt guilty about shit. I did it for my own reasons, but damn," Shakira said.

"Stay away from the bullshit and keep your mouth closed. You have mouths to feed," Shanice said.

"His mom calls every day with the madness. I wish they would find something, just to give her closure," Shakira said.

"How did you do it—and why?" Shanice asked.

"When I came home after I got out of jail, he had stolen my supply, sold it, and gave me what he felt I deserved. Then he talked to bitches in front of me, hit me, and spit in my face. You know he would always come to the house, fuck me, see what he could get out of me, and never touch Gazelle? He did that again. So I took my metal bat and beat the shit out of him. Silas and I threw him in the river," Shakira said.

"Wow, so how do you feel after talking about it? Do you feel that it was justifiable?" Shanice asked.

"I only feel guilty when I am around his family," Shakira said.

"Then stay far away from his family and never speak of this to anyone again." They picked up some food from KFC on the way to Shakira's house. Shakira laid the baby down for the night, and then she and Shanice had a midnight drink and blunt together.

Shakira's phone rang.

"Hey, Sis, turn on the news," Silas said.

"What channel?" she asked.

"Channel Three," he said. Shakira anticipated what it would say. She turned the news on, and the anchor said:

Breaking news: a body was found today in the river just behind the State Street Bridge in Camden, New Jersey. The body, wrapped in thick plastic and duct tape, was found by a young man walking over the bridge as the tide was low today. The body was held by a center block, which was attached to the body by the killer. The coroner has been investigating the scene of the crime all day. The ID of the body is unknown, and there are no suspects at this time.

"Is that him?" Shanice asked.

"Yeah, they found him. The water was supposed to be deep," Shakira said, getting worried.

"The water runs, but it's not deep in those areas. The brick made him settle," Shanice said.

"What am I going to do?" Shakira asked.

"Nothing. No one knows it's him, and he's in another state. Don't say shit, and don't react," Shanice said.

"Silas dumped the truck over here, but I don't know where," Shakira said. Shanice hugged her.

"It's going to be all right, Sis. He's black. What are the odds of them really looking for his killer?" Shanice said.

Shanice stayed at Shakira's that night and left early in the morning to take all the kids to school. Shakira was due at her welfare-to-work program, which she hated. They had to dress up, sit at a computer, and fill out job applications all day. Shakira really wanted to be a paralegal. She had decided to enroll in school months ago, but Steven's nonsense kept distracting her. When she got to the program office that day, she saw a bunch of women dressed in their worst business attire, smelling like perfume from Bath and Bodyworks or Victoria's Secret. Shakira signed herself in for the day and then went to the Community College of Philadelphia to enroll in some classes. Shakira felt like she could finally start something, and finish it without distraction. She only needed a few more credits, but she was scared to start again and not be able to finish. She filled out the application for January and then sat and waited for a counselor to talk with her. The counselor was an elderly white lady with a positive attitude.

"You went here a few years ago finished your first semester full-time, with honors. You ready to enroll again and finish up?" she asked.

"Yes, I am," Shakira said.

"Are you looking to attend full-time again?" the counselor asked.

"Yes, full-time, day attendance," Shakira said. The counselor put two possible schedules together and showed them to Shakira. "This one will get you finished by May of next year. The other schedule will have you done by the end of next year. You can come in early and get out of here by twelve forty-five every afternoon."

"I will take the second schedule and do three classes at a time, because I don't want to set myself up for failure," Shakira said.

The counselor printed out her roster and sent her to financial aid. While there, Shakira filled out an application online. The financial aid advisor gave her a receipt and told her to wait for an award letter in the mail before she registered for classes. Shakira left the school feeling good because she was making a change in her life. As she walked to the parking garage, she heard her phone ring.

"Hello," Shakira said.

Ms. Angie, Steven's mom, said, "Kira Summer is walking around telling people that you know something about Steven's disappearance because he was with you the last time she talked to him."

"He left my house, and I haven't seen him since. Why would I have had something done to him?" Shakira said defensively.

She heard an echo and knew she was on a three-way call, so she decided to throw in a little extra information.

"We fucked that night, and he left after he got a call from someone and told me he would see me in the morning. That bitch is all the way crazy," Shakira said.

"I am just trying to see what happened to my son. I don't really care about y'all's beef. I just want my son to come home alive. I will call you later, Shakira," she said, hanging up. In all the years Ms. Angie had known her, she had never called her Shakira. Shakira felt she was starting to turn on her for Summer, and she needed to fix this problem right away. The last thing she wanted was for Ms. Angie to start snooping around.

Chapter 16

Shanice

Trez had been calling Shanice for weeks to let him see the boys. Shanice finally decided that he could see them soon, but on her terms. She was still angry at the news that Stacy was pregnant, and she didn't want Trez at her house. She called Trez's mom and asked if she could bring the kids to her house to see Trez. His mom loved Shanice and rarely said no to her. Before this meeting, Shanice got her hair and nails done. New hair had grown where the stitches had been, and she got a few tracks to fill in the rest of the bald spot. She knew Trez would be waiting there when they arrived, and she hadn't seen him in weeks, so she made sure that she looked really good. When she pulled up, she saw Trez's truck parked outside. He immediately ran opened his mother's front door from the inside as she pulled up. The boys jumped out of the car and ran to Trez. Shanice stayed in her car as he walked over to her window.

"What's up?" he asked, knocking on the window.

"Nothing, I hear you got a baby on the way," she said, rolling down the window.

"You shouldn't believe everything you hear," he said.

Trez looked at Shanice's eye and saw the remaining scar. It was first time he had seen her up-close since their fight.

"What happened?" he asked, trying to touch her face. She pushed his hand away.

"Stacy has been hiding, and it's pissing me the fuck off," she said.

"What are you talking about?" Trez said.

"Don't act like you don't know. She set me up to be robbed," Shanice said.

"I don't know shit," he said.

"Somebody has to suffer for what I've been through, so you're going to kill her brother for me. If you don't, I will not only get you locked up for my home invasion but also make your little girlfriend and her fetus suffer," she said.

"What?" he said.

"You have until Tuesday. I will pick the boys up on Sunday night." She drove off before he could speak a word, going so fast she nearly ran his feet over. He called her all day after she left, but she ignored the calls.

Shanice stayed in her apartment and waited to catch Stacy creeping into her house. Stacy finally came home around midnight. Shanice waited another hour, until she saw Stacy's bedroom light go off. She took a new towel, wrapped it around a bent hanger, and walked to Stacy's new white Impala. She stuck this device in the gas tank as far as it would go and lit the towel on fire. She walked quickly back to her car a block away. As she got to the end of the block, she heard a loud boom. As she sat in her car and waited for her latest headache to pass, a fire truck sped past her. She drove to her mother's house, where she had been staying. Everyone was sleeping. Shanice sat in the living room and contemplated her next move, waiting to see if Trez would call. He called at six that morning, waking her up.

"Damn, Shanice, I guess you really mean business," he said.

"What are you talking about?" she asked.

"You blew up Stacy's car." he said.

"She should be glad it wasn't her fucking house. The ball's in your court now. No more warnings," she yelled into the phone.

"I got you, Shanice," he said, hanging up.

Shanice never wanted to be with Trez again; she just wanted revenge. She was happy to feel cramps as she got her period. The last thing she wanted was another baby. Soon, Ms. Sandy woke up and came downstairs.

"What are you doing here? I thought you went home," Ms. Sandy said.

"I couldn't sleep."

"You have a lot on your mind. I can see it."

"I am fine," Shanice said.

"No, you're not. I watched the man you ride or die for turn his back on you and sleep with your close friend. Your kids are here more than home, and you're not yourself," Ms. Sandy said.

"Go 'head, Mom. Tell me how you told me so. Despite what everyone thinks, I have feelings. I don't know how to just get over shit. If I suffer, everyone must suffer with me. No one will walk away from this until they have cried more tears than me. I put that on my daddy!" she said, crying. Ms. Sandy grabbed Shanice, hugged her, and cried with her. Shanice didn't usually show emotion—she just lashed out. Today, she had finally opened up to her mother. Ms. Sandy felt good about this. Their moment was interrupted by a loud knock on the door.

"I hope it's not the damn police," Ms. Sandy said, walking to the door.

"Is Shanice Savage here?" Shanice walked to the door, ready to go to jail.

"It's me," she said, putting her hands out.

"You have been served," the officer said. Shanice read the papers and found out that it was a restraining order from Stacy when she pressed charges before. Little Sterling came in after the police left.

"Where have you been all night?" Shanice asked.

"I stayed at Keith's house last night," he answered.

"I better not hear about any girls. School and ball—that's it. Imagine being with a girl as crazy as me," Shanice said, laughing.

"You're my sister that's nasty. Yo, you hear somebody blew up Stacy's car last night?" he said, laughing. Shanice knew that he suspected her, and Ms. Sandy gave her a death stare.

"I think I am going to lie down," Shanice said, dodging her mother's glare. She climbed in bed, popped two Xanax pills, and slept the day away. Later, strong cramps woke her up. She felt wet between her legs and pulled the sheet back to find a pool of bright-red blood.

"Mom, help me!" Shanice screamed. Ms. Sandy and Little Sterling burst into the room.

"Call an ambulance," Ms. Sandy said to her son.

"Calm down, Shanice. It's okay," Ms. Sandy said. Shanice cried her heart out as the pain worsened. The ambulance arrived about twenty minutes later and rushed her to the hospital. Shanice knew she was having a miscarriage. She was tired of being hurt over and over. She was sitting in the ER triage area when Trez called.

"Shanice, what happened? Your brother called me," he said.

"I miscarried," she said.

"It wasn't mine, right?" he asked.

"Why the fuck did you call me? Why the fuck does it matter? It's dead," she said, hanging up.

*   *   *

Trez

"What happened to Shanice?" His mom asked, overhearing his end of the conversation.

"She had a miscarriage," he said.

"Why do you treat her so badly? She loves you, and it shows. I've never seen a girl rock with you like she does. What's going on?" his mother asked.

"I don't know. This shit is crazy," he said.

"What I do know is that little thing staying here every night is trouble, and she and her bad-ass kids gotta go tonight," his mom said.

Trez's phone rang.

"What's up?" Trez said, ignoring his mom as she walked out.

"What's going on?" Jermaine said. "I wanted to put you on this bitch who works with my bitch up at CFCF. She giving a lot of work to that nigga Kyree," Jermaine said.

"Oh really? Kyree is a monster on the streets," Trez said.

"Why go through the trouble of robbing Kyree? I am going to talk my girl into setting her up," Jermaine said.

"Get the info and hit me back," Trez said.

"Solid," Jermaine replied.

Stacey walked into Trez's room as he hung up.

"Your mom's tripping. She knows I can't go home 'cause your baby mom trying to kill me, and she like, 'Get out,'" Stacy said.

"Yo, did you really get Shanice robbed?" he asked.

"Why the fuck do people keep saying that?" she asked. "My brother overheard me talking to her about the money, and he did

97

that on his own. I didn't find out it was him until a week later."
She tried to sound convincing.

"Solid," Trez said.

"What does that mean?" she asked.

"I'm gonna drop you off at home," he said.

"So that's it? I am fucking having your baby." she said,
crying as she held her flat belly.

"You told me that she set that robbery shit up so she could
get attention, but I'm seeing my baby mom walking around,
looking real fucked up for it to be fake shit. I wasn't even taking
her seriously. People have been coming up to me on the street like
I am some fucked-up dude," he said, pointing his finger at her.

"It's not my fucking fault this happened!"

"Bitch, my fucking kids was there! I should beat that fucking
baby out of you. This is your fault!"

Stacy ran down the steps and out of the house in tears. She
walked all the way home with her kids from his mom's house.

Chapter 17

Shante

Harold had been calling Shante and breathing hard all day. They had not seen each other for a while, and she was due to drop the kids off to his mother's for the weekend. Jared had not come over the night before. Shante didn't know if there was anyone else, but she knew that she was not going to take any bullshit from him. She grabbed the kids' belongings and packed them into her truck. Harold's mom lived in the heart of West Philadelphia, not far from the home the couple had shared with each other. His mom was a nice woman with brown skin; short, curly white hair; and flawless skin. She was always overdressed, with long nails and plenty of makeup. She also knew her son was an asshole. She loved Shante and asked her to come in for a while when she dropped the kids off. Shante was hesitant, but she went inside as the kids unpacked and ran straight to the basement where all the toys and the TV were. The women sat in the kitchen, and Harold's mother poured them each a Long Island Iced Tea.

"What happened? Why did you leave?" she asked.

"The cheating, verbal abuse, and sometimes physical abuse," Shante said in tears.

"I can't blame you for that. But he told me you withheld sex as a punishment, and that's why he cheated."

"No, I withheld sex because he cheated and gave me an STD."

"Is counseling an option?" his mother asked.

Shante laughed. "I moved out, and I am filing for divorce. I am happy with my decision. I do not want to be with your son, and that's it," she said.

"Enough said. I told him I would talk to you, but I know what you're going through. Another woman came to my house, hollering about being pregnant. Do what you must. I know you're a good woman. Just don't take the kids away," his mother said. She put her glass up for a toast. "To new beginnings."

Shante cut her visit short after noticing that it was three in the afternoon, and she had not received a phone call from Jared yet. She called him from the car, and he picked up on the first ring.

"Where are you?" she asked.

"I stayed home. I had to handle some business," he said.

"Oh really?" she said. "I just dropped off the kids. Can we have dinner?" she asked.

"Yes, I can meet you at Coo's for a drink in an hour," he said. Shante went home and got dressed. She got there first and waited forty minutes after he was supposed to be there. After having two drinks, she had had enough. He walked in as she was walking out. He hurried behind her. He pulled on her arm, and she turned around.

"What the fuck? Jared, is this too much for you? Just let me know," she said.

"I am sorry, Shante. I had some business that I wanted to take care of," he said.

"What business?" Shante asked.

"Shante, you already know," he said.

"Don't tell me that you're selling drugs. You have a bright future," she said and turned to walk away. He grabbed her and hugged her tight.

"Don't be my teacher—be my girl. Tell me that it's okay to make a way for us," he said.

"I care too much about you to see you mess up your life," she said, pulling away and walking to her car.

"I am not going to get caught. I don't sell anything hand in hand. I just distribute," he said, following her.

"Whatever, Jared." She got in her car to drive off.

"Don't just throw us away! Please, meet me at the house. I will follow you there," he pleaded before she left.

Shante sped home, and Jared was right behind her. She ran into the house and tried to walk straight to the bedroom. He pulled her hand and turned her around.

"Shante, how can I afford to help you if I don't do this? I don't want to watch you struggle. I want to take care of you and be with you," he said, pouring stacks of money out of a duffel bag. He kissed her as he walked her into the kitchen. Shante was speechless. More than anything, she just wanted to be loved. He took her shirt off and kissed her on her neck and breasts. He pulled her pants down and put her on the marble countertop. He pulled her knee boots and pants off. He put his head between her legs and pushed her panties to the side as his tongue stroked inside her until she creamed. He then pulled her off the countertop, bent her over the stove, and let himself melt inside her. They both fell on the kitchen floor. Shante forgot what she was mad about. They spent the weekend in bed, admiring each other and talking. Shante found out that Jared loved her more than she thought. He was more than a young lover. He was the man that Harold had been before he became an asshole. She decided to let him be a man, and she would be his woman, not a teacher.

It was Sunday morning already, and Shante was ready to pick the kids up at Harold's mother's house, but Harold told her to pick them up at his house because his mom was staying late at church. Jared was out for the morning to shoot hoops with his friends, and Shante didn't want to bug him with her drama. She looked at the gun in her drawer and then grabbed her Taser instead, for protection in case Harold started tripping. She hated him so much.

Jared had taken her truck, so she had no choice but to drive his Infiniti. "I always wondered how he could afford this car," she said under her breath. She walked up to the door at Harold's house, prepared to use her key. Laughing, she decided to ring the doorbell. Harold came to the door in a navy-blue robe smelling of funk and liquor.

"Where are the kids?" she asked.

"They are on their way. I didn't expect you so soon, but we need to talk," he said, closing the door behind her.

"I don't have anything to talk to you about. I am just here for my kids. I will wait in the car," she said. Harold blocked the door.

"I am sorry, Shante. I miss you. Can we work this out? I am nothing without you," he said.

"You should have said that six months ago, before I fell in love with someone who is more of a man than you will ever be," she said, grabbing the doorknob.

"Fell in love? That's a fucking little boy you have around my kids. You've been screwing this nigga all this time. I knew you were a whore," he said, getting mad.

"A whore? You started the bullshit. Good-bye, Harold. Call your mom and tell her I am on my way," she said.

She grabbed her pocketbook and reached for her Taser. She reached for the door with the other hand and opened it, but he slammed it closed. He grabbed her by the neck, knocking her purse out of her hand and pushing her to the floor. He got on top of her and kissed her face all over.

"You are going to love me again, Shante," he said.

He pulled down her pants and panties, holding her hands tightly with one of his hands. He put himself inside of her, biting her face as she tried to fight him off. She screamed, and he covered her mouth with his other hand. He began to move inside of her quickly. In less than a minute, he said, "This pussy is so good, yes!" as he ejaculated inside of her. Shante felt like she left her body at that moment. She lay there on the floor in what had been her living room a month before. Harold rolled off to the floor alongside of her, as if what had just happened was okay. Shante came back to her senses and grabbed her pocketbook. She picked up the Taser and looked at Harold, naked except for his robe. She aimed the weapon straight at his balls. She watched as he screamed and convulsed.

He immediately balled up into a fetal position as she ran to leave. But he grabbed her feet, and she fell and hit the floor. "I am going to fucking kill you," Harold yelled. Shante ran for the kitchen and grabbed the first knife she saw. It was a small but sharp knife, almost like a dagger. She stabbed him in the face and then in the neck, and blood squirted all over her clothes.

She stabbed him over and over in the neck and chest until she no longer felt movement from him.

"I hate you!" she screamed and then stomped on his face. She saw herself in the mirror and noticed that she looked like a monster. Shante stopped crying and looked at what she had done. Blood was all over. She immediately came to her senses when she heard police sirens nearby. She washed the knife off and put it in her pocketbook along with the Taser. She ran upstairs and tried to keep from touching anything as she took a shower and threw on some clothes she had left there. She found a pair of flip-flops in the closet. She threw the bloody clothes and shoes in a trash bag and took it with her. She washed his private area, trying to get her DNA off of him. She wiped down everything she had touched, including the front door. She didn't park in front of his door, and she didn't drive her own car, so she hoped no one could say that they had seen her there. She drove to her mother's house and noticed all her sisters' cars were there, which reminded her that it was time for Sunday family dinner. She fixed herself up the best that she could. She ran straight to the bathroom, sat down, and cried her eyes out. Shanice knocked on the door.

"Are you okay, Sis?" she asked.

"Yeah," Shante said, trying to hide that she was crying.

"No, you're not. What's wrong?" Shanice asked. Shante opened the door, revealing her bitten face and disheveled look.

"What happened?"

"Harold raped me."

"He did what?" Shanice said, instantly getting angry. She text-messaged Shayla and Shakira. They both came upstairs, and Shante told them what Harold did to her.

"I fucking hate Harry. Wait till I fucking see his ass again. I am going to light him on fire," Shanice said.

"I killed him," Shante whispered.

"You did what!" Shayla said.

"That's my fucking girl. Fuck Harry," Shanice said.

"What about the kids? He was a good father," Shante said.

"If he was really a good father, he wouldn't keep hurting his kid's mother," Shayla said.

"You know we've got your back if you need us," Shakira said.

Shante changed into some of Shanice's clothes and did her hair and makeup. She pulled herself together, and Shanice drove her back to Harold's house as if she was going to get the kids now.

"Remember, you're just getting here. He texted you to pick up the kids, and you said okay," Shanice said, preparing Shante for the situation.

She then called Harold's mother, pretending she did not know what was going on. His mother met her at the house with the kids.

Shante said, "I have been calling him and ringing the bell. He told me you wanted me to pick the kids up here." She tried to keep herself together.

"He's probably in there drunk, trying to get you over here," his mom said.

The kids ran to greet Shante.

"Let me go check on him," Harold's mom said.

Shante took a deep breath and told her kids to get in the car as she heard his mother scream.

"What's wrong?" Shante said, running to the door. Harold was still laid out on the floor, covered with blood. Shante could not hold in her emotions, and she cried at what she had done.

Shanice called the police, and there were cops and reporters there in minutes. Shanice took the kids to Ms. Sandy's house, and Shante stuck around to see what would happen.

Shante left a voice mail for Jared, saying, "This is Shante. There has been an accident. Someone killed Harold. Call me when you can."

By the time Shante got back to her mother's house to get the kids, they were sleeping. The cops didn't want to question her at the moment, but she knew their questions would come soon.

Shakira, Shanice, and Shayla had waited up for her.

"Are you okay?" Shakira asked.

"Yeah. I know I did what I had to, but I feel so bad for my kids. Now I have to tell them that their father is dead," she answered.

"Whatever happens, stick to your story. You have to be here for your kids," Shanice said.

Chapter 18

Shayla

It had been a while since Shayla had heard from Hick. She turned the prepaid phone on just to see if he had left any messages. There were twenty messages, and Shayla listened to the last one. In it, Hick said:

You stupid bitch. I would have left her to be with you. You took my money. You didn't pay my lawyer. Do you think I will be in jail forever? You won't know when I get out, and you'd better watch your back. I am going to make you suffer—it's about to get really personal.

Shayla hung up the phone as tears fell from her eyes. She felt sick to her stomach, so she ran to the bathroom and gagged over the toilet.

"You still want me to take you to the market?" Kyree asked, walking upstairs. Kyree had been staying with Shayla since the basketball was left on the steps, but she was hiding her pregnancy from him.

"Yeah, I need to grab a few things for New Year's Eve at my mom's." Shayla grabbed her coat and keys. They left together in her Range Rover. Shayla wanted to buy the food at a store close to her mom's house so that she could drop it off and see her. Kyree dropped her off at the front door of the market and parked. Shayla walked into the store with a hood over her head and picked up the food as quickly as possible. When she got outside, she noticed she had left her phone in the car and was unable to call Kyree to come get her there. Two men with hoods jumped on Shayla, and she screamed for help. She reached for her gun, but it was hard to get to, inside her purse. One of the men put a gun to Shayla's head.

"Make your last wish," he said as he pulled the trigger. Pop, pop! The gunmen fell to the ground as another man with a ski mask over his face grabbed her. She knew it was Kyree because she smelled his cologne. More shots were fired, and people screamed as Kyree held Shayla in a headlock and protected her and brought her back to the car. Pop, pop, pop! Kyree fired more shots as he opened the back passenger door, threw her in, and slammed it. Shayla curled up in the backseat and heard more gunshots. Kyree got in the car and sped off.

"Shay, you all right, boo? Let me get you out of here," he said. Then he immediately got on the phone.

"Yo, man, where the fuck you at? Shit just got real. It's gotta be some niggas from across town. I just took out like four niggas. I gotta hide my people. We're in defense mode now. Get the Goons ready," he said. Shayla was scared. She felt like she had started an unnecessary war because she was a scorned woman. Kyree took her to the Marriot in Center City until he could get things in order.

"No one in my family can know about this. I have to go to my mom's on Friday for New Year's Eve like this never happened," Shayla said.

"You don't want to take that shit to your mom's crib," Kyree said.

"I cannot miss it. I do not know how many days are promised to me," she said.

"I got your back," Kyree said. Shayla threw up in the bathroom.

"You ain't pregnant, are you?" Kyree said.

"What?" she said defensively.

"Well, at least I know it's not mine. You keep playing hard to get," he said. "Are you hungry?"

"No, how can you eat like you didn't just kill people?" Shayla asked.

"I am a fucking killer. You don't believe the stories?" he asked.

"Yeah, I've heard some shit," she said. "You remind me of my daddy. I saw him do a lot of shit to people. It fucked me up and made me want a man who was a mean as my daddy and who takes care of business like him. But it only ever got me men who lie, cheat, and break my heart," Shayla continued.

"I am nothing like that. What you see is what you get from me. I don't have a girl because I like to fuck pussy with no strings attached. I take what I want when I want it, with no remorse," Kyree said.

"Whatever," she replied.

"What, I know you're not catching feelings?" he asked.

"No, I am not," she said.

"I am all wrong for you. I can protect you and do business with you, but I can't love you," he said.

Shayla's phone rang with a call from Shanice.

"Hello," Shayla said.

"I just heard that you're fucking Kyree, and he was just in a shootout over some money and you were there. What the fuck is going on?" she asked.

"It's true, and I am fine. Please don't say a word to anyone else," Shayla asked.

"Are you going to be at Mom's tomorrow?" Shanice asked.

"Yeah, but I need you to take her shopping 'cause I won't be able too. I will pay you back," Shayla said.

"I got it, Sis, but you'd better tell me what's going on," Shanice said, hanging up.

"Everything cool?" Kyree asked.

"Yeah, I am cool," Shayla said.

Kyree took a call and ran into the hall for privacy. He came back with a funny look on his face.

"Is everything okay? You look funny. Did some baby mama cuss you out?" she asked.

"You know how chicks are," he said, laughing it off.

"I am so glad I didn't give you any of these yams. I think I am ready to go to sleep," she said. "Can you pick me up tomorrow afternoon? I am going to need a rental car. My dad's people are picking up the Range Rover to chop it up tonight. I am so glad that car was in Hick's name," she said, getting under the blanket and turning on a movie. Kyree looked surprised.

"Don't be shocked, boo. I was my dad's clean-up person," she said.

"You want me to check on the house?" he asked.

"No, I have security set up through my phone. I don't want to put you in any more danger," Shayla said. Something about Kyree's expression made Shayla think he was hiding something.

Chapter 19

New Year's Eve

The whole family was at Ms. Sandy's house for New Year's Eve. The spread filled the dining room table, and there was plenty of liquor. Everyone was having a good time.

"What time is it?" Shakira asked Shante.

"It's eleven thirty already," Shante said, looking at her watch.

"Where is Little Sterling? He should have been home from his game by now," Shakira said. "Sterling ain't here yet?" Ms. Sandy asked.

"No," Shakira said. Ms. Sandy called his phone, and he didn't answer. She called repeatedly and began to panic.

"Sterling just ran upstairs," Silas yelled.

"He's upstairs, Mommy," Shakira said, repeating Silas.

"Okay," Ms. Sandy said, yelling over the noise.

It was midnight, and New Year's Day had begun. Ms. Sandy looked around for all her children, so she could give them all hugs and kisses. It made her feel good to start the year with her kids.

"Tell Sterling to get his ass downstairs," Ms. Sandy yelled to Silas, who was standing near the steps. He ran upstairs to look for his brother, but Sterling was nowhere to be found.

"Mommy, he's not here," Silas said as he ran back downstairs. Shayla picked up her phone to call Little Sterling.

"Hello," said the voice on the other end.

"Hello, Sterling. Where the fuck are you?" she asked.

"The question is, where the fuck are you, Shayla?" said the voice.

"Excuse me?" she said.

"You took something important to Hick, and now I have something important to you," the voice said.

"What?" she said.

"I have your little ball player. If you want him back alive, go to the door, get the note off the porch, and follow the directions, or else he dies," the voice said before hanging up. Shayla ran to the door with Silas close behind her. On the porch, there was a bloody basketball jersey that little Sterling had worn earlier. Silas snatched the note. He read, "Shayla, you know what this is about. Bring three hundred fifty thousand dollars and the number to the connect, or your little ball player will die tonight. I will call with the location at one."

"What the fuck is going on?" Silas asked.

"Um." Shayla tried to get her words together and then started screaming.

"Fuck all that shit. They got our little bro. What the fuck did you do?" he asked, shaking her roughly. She fell to the porch floor in shock and threw up. Shanice, Shakira, and Shante went outside, and Shante knelt down and hugged Shayla.

"What is going on?" Shanice asked.

"This stupid bitch did some shit. Now someone has our fucking brother and wants three hundred fifty grand for him! Where are we supposed to get that type of money?" Silas asked.

"What is going on, Shay?" Shante asked.

"Fuck that. Get up, bitch." Silas grabbed her and threw her against the wall.

"Where the fuck is my brother?" he yelled. Shayla just cried harder.

"Get the fuck off my sister," Shante yelled, pulling on Silas.

"Look at this shit," Silas said, showing them the letter.

"You gotta tell us something, Sis, so we can help," Shakira said.

"Help? She better have everything they want, 'cause I am fucked up. If my fucking brother dies, so will you." Silas screamed as he walked off.

Shayla said, "I took some money and drugs from Hick after I found out he had a wife and kids. I got her address and had a talk with her. Yesterday, two Hispanic guys tried to kill me, and Kyree killed them before they got to me."

"Wait, you're fucking Kyree?" Shanice asked.

"No, he's just getting rid of the shit for me," Shayla said. "I have been in contact with the connect since Hick was locked up. He does not want to do business with Hick anymore."

"So you never heard the story of how Hick killed Kyree's little brother to get to his connect?" Shanice asked.

"Hick and Kyree have both mentioned it," Shayla said.

"You just started a war. Hick hates Kyree. He always said that Kyree had his own brother killed," Shanice said.

"Hick won't be getting out anytime soon," Shayla said.

"Do you have the money they need?" Shakira said.

"Yes, I have it in a safe and in some accounts," she said.

"Don't do anything without insurance. Where's his bitch?" Shanice asked.

"She lives near Franklin Mills," Shayla answered.

"What time is it?" Shanice said.

"Twelve fifteen. We can make it up there," Shakira said.

"Wherever they meet us, they'd better bring our brother," Shakira said. The girls jumped into Shayla's rental truck. Shanice had a lead foot on the way to Shayla's house to pick up some guns. Shayla gave all her sisters a hand gun from the collection Hick had left at her house before he was sent to prison. They jumped on the expressway and arrived at Samantha's house in no time.

"What time is it?" Shanice asked.

"Twelve fifty," Shayla replied.

"Two in the front and two in the back," Shanice said. She went to the front door with Shayla, who reached to ring the doorbell.

"What the fuck are you doing?" Shanice asked.

"Ringing the bell," Shayla said.

"Bitch, this is a home invasion," Shanice said.

"She has an alarm. You'll at least want her to disarm it," Shayla said.

"Fuck that shit," Shanice said. She kicked in the door, and Hick's wife was sitting on the couch, holding her baby. The infant started to cry.

"Put the fucking baby in the bassinet," Shanice said, pointing the gun at Samantha.

"Okay, okay," she said. As she did what they demanded, she picked up a silver .22 from the coffee table and pointed it at Shayla and Shanice.

"Y'all shouldn't leave your doors open in the suburbs," Shakira said, walking up behind Samantha and pointing a gun at the back of her head. Shante took the gun from Samantha and pushed her onto the couch.

"I know that you know who has my little brother," Shayla said.

"You should have let this be when I told you it was bigger than you. My family feels like they owe Hick now because he helped them when they needed it," she said in her Spanish accent.

"Fuck that. Your family has my brother. Call them and tell them to give him back," Shayla said.

"No, I won't be involved. A lot of my family's blood was shed yesterday. Three of my brothers were killed over ghetto trash," Samantha said, looking at Shayla.

"You already are involved," Shanice said she pulled the clip out and hit Samantha in the head with the gun twice. Shayla's phone rang.

"Hello," Shayla said. She put the call on speaker phone.

"Do you have the money? No, I have Hick's wife and kids. If he wants them back alive, my brother had better come back alive too," Shayla said. The caller hung up.

"What happened?" Shanice said.

"I don't know," Shayla answered.

"Okay, put this bitch in the trunk, lock the doors, and leave the kids," Shanice said.

"You're just gonna leave the kids?" Shakira said.

"Bitch, I ain't fucking with kids," Shanice said. They put Samantha in the trunk and went back to north Philadelphia as they waited outside of Shakira's house in silence for a phone call. It was four in the morning, and the people who had taken Little Sterling still hadn't called back yet. However, Ms. Sandy had been calling the girls all night.

"We have to go and tell Mommy something. She is freaking out," Shante said.

"Okay, we will take this bitch to one of Shayla's properties and take turns watching her until we hear something," Shanice said.

"Take turns? Y'all know I have enough going on," Shante said.

"Yeah, take fucking turns. We all in this shit together, hon," Shanice said.

"Where the fuck is Silas? He can take the first shift while we talk to Mommy," Shanice said.

Shakira called him and said, "I am going to text you an address. Meet us there in ten minutes."

"He said okay," Shakira told her sisters. The girls went to a property under renovation that Shayla had just purchased. Samantha's head was covered with Shanice's coat, so she could not see where they were. They picked her up and carried her into the house and straight to the back room, where they tied her to a chair and taped her mouth shut. Her head continued to bleed, and she didn't cry or yell at all. Silas came to the house dressed in black and mad at the world. He walked straight past Shayla with a look of hate.

"What the fuck is going on?" he asked.

"We have Hick's wife as collateral so that he will return Sterling in one piece," Shanice said. "But we need you to watch her while we go talk to Mommy."

"How do you know they haven't killed him already?" Silas asked.

"We don't know. But if they do, kill her," Shanice said. She took Shante's gun and passed it to him. The sisters went to Ms. Sandy's house. She was sitting on the porch with worry in her eyes, and she walked to the car, looking for Sterling, as they parked.

"Where is my baby? What happened?" Ms. Sandy asked in tears. The girls walked over and hugged their mother.

"We are going to get him back," Shakira said.

"We promise," Shanice added.

* * *

Hick

Samantha's brother, Hector, paced the warehouse as he waited for Hick's call. Little Sterling was blindfolded and secured to a chair with duct tape. His face was bloody from the beating he got when Hector found out that his sister was kidnapped. Finally, the phone rang.

"What the fuck do you mean, 'They got my wife'? Those bitches ain't even built like that," Hick said, screaming in the phone.

"What you want us to do with the kid? If we kill him, they will kill her," Hector said.

"Y'all were supposed to be watching her! Fuck that. Give the kid back—blow off his kneecaps and throw him in the ER. I will deal with this bitch when I get out," Hick said.

"What about the money? I lost three of my brothers yesterday, trying to kidnap this bitch," Hector said.

"Fuck the money. They got my wife! Give them what they want. That's what happens in the game. You win some, you lose some," Hick said.

"What!" Hector shouted.

"I will call tomorrow. It's getting hot in here, with this phone. Y'all better have Samantha back by then," Hick said.

Hector hung up the phone and picked up a shotgun.

"This is for Sammy." Hector shot Sterling in the right knee, and he screamed. He reloaded the gun and shot Sterling in the left knee.

"Please, help!" Sterling screamed.

Sterling's other captor beat him with a metal bat until he stopped screaming.

"I hope he's dead. Let's put him in the truck," said Hector

They drove him to Temple University Hospital as he continued to scream in pain. They stopped and threw him out of the truck, and he rolled down the hill and into the ER. Hector called Shayla's phone, and Shanice answered.

"He's at Temple. Where can I get my sister?" Hector asked.

"You don't get her until we find out if our brother is really alive," Shanice said, hanging up.

"What are you doing? Let her go," Shayla said.

"No, fuck that. You started this shit over some dick, and you're spending money on Range Rovers and shit. I don't know if my fucking brother is alive. Until then, that bitch can rot!" Shanice said.

"We're not gangsters, bitch. You are acting crazy," Shayla said.

"No, bitch, we're not gangsters—we're fucking Savages, and I will kill for all of mine," Shanice replied. Ms. Sandy and all the girls ran to the car. They were at the hospital within minutes.

Shakira found the nurse's station and said, "We're looking for a male patient. He was just dropped off here. His name is Sterling."

"A kid in the back said his name was Sterling," said a nurse. "He's in trauma care now. They are stabilizing him. One of you can come back to ID him, but you can't stay."

"I will go," Shanice said.

Sterling had tubes in his mouth and blood all over his body. Shaniece saw his face and nodded to indicate that it was him as she cried. She ran out to tell the others, still in tears.

Chapter 20

Shakira

Shakira had not slept in three days when she finally went home to get more clothes and check on a few things. Little Sterling was still in critical condition, and Shanice would not let Hick's wife go. Shakira was due to take a shift that night, so she decided to get some sleep. Her phone rang. It was Mika calling.

"Hello," Shakira said.

"I've been trying to call you. I am so sorry about what happened to your brother," Mika said. "He's in critical but stable condition. He needed three surgeries, and he may never walk again," Shakira said as tears began to fall.

"Are you going to be okay?" Mika asked.

"Yeah, we're good," Shakira answered.

"I hate to bring it up at a time like this, but I talked to Nikko last night, and she told me you've been buying pills off of her," Mika said.

"Yeah, she was selling them," Shakira said.

"You know that's my connect. She said you called her up and asked her to let you know first when she got pills, and you would have a bonus for her," Mika said.

"What are you getting at?" Shakira said.

"Bitch, you stepped on my fucking toes. You stole my connect and clients after I looked the fuck out for you," Mika said.

"It's just business," Shakira replied.

"Fuck all that shit. You're lucky you're my son's aunt, or else—"

"Or else what? I know you ain't throwing threats this way," Shakira said.

"What the fuck are you gonna do, bitch? I've got some shit on you that will send you away for the rest of your life," Mika said.

"What the fuck does that mean?" Shakira asked.

"Silas told me about what happened the night that Steven went missing. I wondered why he was driving around that night in his truck," Mika said.

"You're threatening my freedom with some bullshit?" Shakira said angrily.

"Ha, yeah, bitch. Squirm like the worm you are," Mika said, laughing. Shakira hung up, threw her phone on the bed, and screamed.

"Fucking Silas, I hate you!" she yelled.

Shakira tossed her room upside down to alleviate some anger and then cried herself to sleep. She woke up at seven in the evening, and it had already been dark for a few hours. She was still beyond angry with Silas. Mika was now a threat to her and her kids. She hated the thought of killing her friend and hoped that Silas could fix this problem. She dialed his number as she sat on the toilet, smoking a Newport cigarette.

"Yo, Sis," Silas yelled when he answered the phone.

"Explain to me how your bitch knows about Steven?" she asked.

"Sis, don't worry about her. She told me about your little conversation earlier. She ain't gonna say anything. If you go down, I go down, right?" he said.

"If I go down, she goes down. Check your bitch or bury her," Shakira said.

"Damn, Sis. All this over some pills? Y'all supposed to be best friends," Silas said.

"It's about respect. She threatened my freedom. So you'd better check that bitch before I do," Shakira repeated.

"Sis, you ain't gotta worry," Silas said.

"I can't believe you're a pillow-talking ass nigga. I told you about that shit," she said.

"Bye, Sis," he said, hanging up. As Shakira got dressed to relieve Shanice, she called her mom up to check on Little Sterling.

Ms. Sandy picked up on the first ring.

She said, "He's still sleeping. They are talking about amputating his legs because there's no circulation in them. They want me to make a decision."

"Where's Shante?" Shakira asked.

"She went to watch the kids so Shayla can come here with me," Ms. Sandy said.

"I will be there in the morning," Shakira said.

"I love you, baby. Be safe," Ms. Sandy said in tears.

"I love you too," Shakira said.

Shakira cried hard for a few more minutes before she pulled herself together. Her mother was hurt. Shakira was angry, and someone was going to pay. She jumped in her car and cruised over to the rental property. She went in through the back door and walked straight to the room where they were holding Samantha. Crack! Shakira punched her hard on the right side of her face. Shanice ran into the room.

"Oh, girl, I thought the bitch got away," she said, walking back to the other room. Shanice had set up shop with her portable TV and DVD player. She was smoking a blunt, as usual.

"Did you bring food?" Shanice asked.

"Yeah, here it is," Shakira said, passing her a McDonald's bag.

"Good, I was starving. I am going home to take a shower as soon as possible. I saw a rat as big as a mommy cat, and there are spiders for days in here. I wonder what that bitch was planning on doing with this place," Shanice said.

"I don't know. But I know she's sitting on some money and always acting like she's broke," Shakira said, sitting down at the table set that the previous owners left.

Shanice said, "I hate her for the shit that's happening to us. I talked to her last night.

"'When we gonna let the wife go? We have Sterling back now,' Shayla said to me.

"'When he comes out of his coma,' I told her.

"'That could be weeks from now,' she said.

"'Yeah, so what?' I asked.

"'You're taking this too far,' she said.

"I told her, 'You dumb bitch, you took it too far when you stole Hick's drugs and money because he had a wife. Then you were dumb enough to think that your pussy was so good that he would not retaliate. Now I'm stuck cleaning up your mess.'"

Shakira laughed and said, "Silas and her, always with the crazy shit. Our brother went and told Mika about what happened with Steven," Shakira said.

"What!" Shanice said, covering her mouth.

"The bitch called my house and threatened to rat me out to the police, so I told Silas he better get it under control," Shakira explained.

"You believe that shit?" Shanice asked, taking a drag of her blunt.

"He'd better fix it," Shakira said.

"You gonna wait on Silas, the worst fuckup of all, to fix something? I'll bet that she won't rat you out to the cops, but she probably told her friend, who told somebody who knows his mom or that other chick he got pregnant," Shanice said.

Shakira sat there in a daze for a moment and then said, "I gotta take her out."

Shanice took a long drag of her blunt before answering, "No, you don't. Make Silas do it. Fuck his baby mom. He shouldn't have told her, and she's a threat."

Shakira knew Shanice was right, but she hated the thought of killing someone else. Silas made a mess of even little shit, and this was really going to be difficult for him to do. She decided to contemplate it a little longer. Shanice and Shakira laughed and joked as they shared a blunt and watched *Martin*.

"I have to pick up the boys and take them to Trez," Shanice said after a while.

Samantha moaned. "Let me the fuck out of here!" she yelled.

"Bitch, shut the fuck up!" Shanice yelled back.

"Have y'all been feeding her?" Shakira asked.

"Ha, you feed her. I am leaving," Shanice replied.

"She's been here three days," Shakira said.

"She will die of dehydration and starvation or a bullet to the head. If Sterling doesn't make it, neither will she," Shanice said.

"Have you heard from her peeps?" Shakira asked.

"No. Let Shayla deal with that shit," Shanice answered.

"I think I just broke her jaw," Shakira admitted.

"Yeah, well, she will be all right," Shanice said, walking out the door with her pocketbook.

Chapter 21

Shanice

After Shanice took a shower, she lay down to get a few hours of sleep before taking the kids to Trez's mom's house for a few days. Before she fell asleep, her phone rang.

"Hello," she said.

"Open the door," said the voice on the phone.

"Who the fuck is this?" she asked.

"Trez," he said. She jumped up, wearing only black boy shorts and a tank top. She ran down the steps and opened the door. It had been a long time since Trez had knocked on her door.

He walked in and said, "I am sorry, Shanice. That bitch lied and screwed up my head. She told me you were messing with all these dudes and that you lied about the robbery. I believed her."

"Is that supposed to make shit better? I told you what I wanted," Shanice said.

"I took care of that. You gonna hear about it soon," he said.

"Okay, I feel a little better. You can pick up the kids at my mom's tomorrow," she said, opening the front door so he would leave.

"Wait, I need a favor. Let me go get the guns I left here," he said.

"They're right where you left them," she replied. Shanice sat on the couch as he went to the basement. Soon, he came upstairs with a duffel bag and dropped it on the living room floor.

"My man put me on this dude, Kyree, who's eating off a chick who has a connect with some coke," Trez said, pulling guns out the bag.

"What if I said I know exactly who you're talking about," she said.

"Tell me more," he said.

"No, first I need you to handle my business. I get fifty percent of everything—coke or money," she said.

He made a phone call and asked, "Is it done yet?"

As soon as he hung up, he said, "It's done."

"How do I know you're not lying?" she said.

"You'll hear the sirens in a minute."

She looked out the window and saw a police car and an ambulance pass her house and go directly toward Stacy's.

"Her brother has been staying at her apartment. They ran up in her shit just like they did to you," Trez explained.

Shanice smiled at this good news.

"How is your brother doing?" Trez asked.

"He's hanging on. We are still waiting for him to wake up," she said.

"I am so sorry. I want us to be like we were before," he said.

"We can never be like that again. I do not ever want to be with you. You are my kids' father, and you're only alive now because they love you," said Shanice. Trez looked completely shocked.

"It's like that?" he asked.

She looked him straight in the eye and crossed her arms. "Yes. All this shit has made me grow up. I have made sacrifices for so many people, and they only throw me to the wolves. I don't feel for anyone but my kids and certain people in my family. Enough of the bullshit. Let's get back to business." She pulled away from him and held back her tears.

Trez had a tear in one of his eyes too. He felt her anger toward him and knew that after all the years of back and forth, they were finally over.

"I've got five hundred for you," he said, pulling out five hundred-dollar bills. She took it quickly.

"The kids could use some things, but I am worth more than your money can buy. Now, back to business. I am going with this chick tomorrow night to pick up the drugs. I will text you from a prepaid phone with the apartment address tomorrow, and then I will text you again when we are on our way there. Wait for us to get there before you do anything. You don't need a gang of niggas, just you and maybe two other people. The girl does not die—just knock her out, you got it?" said Shanice.

"Yeah, I got it," he said.

"Make sure that when you leave this time, you take all your shit. There is no coming back. If you try to burn me, I will be your worst enemy," she said as she drank a glass of water in the kitchen. Trez put his guns back in the duffel bag, and she gave him trash bags from under the sink to put his clothes in. She took her wig off and sat down, as she felt a headache coming. She took a couple of pain pills, knowing they would knock her out for a few hours. She grabbed a blanket and listened to Trez gather his belongings.

"Are you okay?" Trez asked when he came downstairs with three full trash bags.

"Yeah, it's just a little headache," she said.

"You gonna call me tomorrow right?" he asked.

"I said I would. Please take your kids to your mom's in the morning. I kinda need a break with all the shit going on," she said.

"I will pick them up first thing tomorrow," he agreed, opening the door. "You sure you don't want me to stay and help you?"

"No, you did enough," she said sarcastically.

"I love you, Shanice. I am going to make it up to you."

"Yeah, sure, whatever."

Chapter 22

Shante

"Sit your ass down now. It's nap time," Shante yelled. All of her sisters' kids were at her house, and they were driving her crazy. She hadn't seen or heard from Jared since the incident with her brother a few days before, but he had been calling her like crazy. She knew that her life was becoming too much for him to handle.

"If I have to tell you one more time, I am going to kick your ass," she yelled at the children. A knock at the door made everyone quiet down.

"Who is it?" she asked in total distress.

"Jared!" he said from behind the door.

She opened the door, trying to hide the fact that she looked a mess.

"I miss you, baby," he said. She smiled.

"My family has been going through so much, and I really don't want to involve you in our drama," she said.

"Can I come in? It's cold out here," he said.

"Are you sure you want to? Excuse the mess. I am on mommy duty," she said, letting him in.

"These are all my nieces and nephews," Shante said, walking into the living room, where all the children were sitting on the floor. "You guys can go upstairs for a little while," she suggested to the kids.

"How is your brother doing?" he asked.

"He is fine right now. He had so many surgeries. He wanted to play ball, and he was so good at it, but he may never walk again. Now we are just waiting for him to wake up," she said as tears rolled down her cheeks. Jared hugged her tightly, and she cried in his arms. "I am okay. I know he will be fine," she said after a few moments, wiping her face.

"What about Harold?" Jared asked.

"The funeral is tomorrow, and the kids are hanging in there. They lost their dad, and their uncle is still in bad shape. It's a mess," she said, in tears again. "How have you been?" she asked, changing the subject.

"I have been a little stressed out," he said.

"I hope that's not because of me," she said.

"No, I have been going through my own shit. My big sister is missing. I can't get any info from anyone about where she is. I've been going crazy, and I kind of needed my baby to be here for me." He hugged her tighter and kissed her.

"You never told me you had a sister," she said.

"Yeah, we are really close. They said she got up and left her kids one night. But I know it's more than that. My dad and her husband are both in the game. Her brothers are not mine, but we all grew up together. If it were simple, my dad wouldn't be so mad right now. Her husband is cool—that's who I get coke from. My dad doesn't know I am dealing. He just wants me to play ball and go to school. As wicked as it sounds, I want to be just like him instead of LeBron James," he said. Shante laughed.

"I have never heard that before. I hope they find your sister," said Shante.

"Her husband is supposed to be handling it, but if he doesn't tell me something soon, I am going to step in."

"Let him handle it. You have so much to look forward to instead of worrying about this. She left on her own, so she will come back the same way, especially for her kids."

"She just had my niece Molly a few weeks ago," he said.

"She may have postpartum depression. Just give it some time," Shante said.

The kids ran downstairs. Dallas, Shakira's son, said, "Grandma's on the phone." He handed Shante the phone.

"Hello," said Ms. Sandy.

"Hi, Mom. What's up?" Shante asked.

"He woke up!" Ms. Sandy said.

"He woke up!" Shante yelled, and all the kids cheered. "Can I talk to him?" Shante asked her mom.

"He's not saying much now. They are going to run a few tests," Ms. Sandy said.

"Tell him I love him, and I will be there soon," Shante said, hanging up.

"I am glad that one of us got good news," Jared said, hugging her again.

"Everything will be okay. Don't worry," she said.

"I am going to leave. I see your hands are full. Can I see you tonight? I need you," Jared said.

"Yeah, but it might be late tonight. I want to see my brother and know that he's okay," she said.

"We can talk later. I need to make a few calls about the sis," he said.

"Okay. I love you, Jared. I hope everything will be okay," she said, kissing him on the lips.

As he left, a detective walked up to the door.

"You must be Shante," he said.

"Who wants to know?" Shante asked.

"I am Detective Woods. I have a few questions about what happened the day Harold was found dead."

"Okay," Shante replied as her heart sank to her feet. But then she remembered what Shanice told her to say.

"He texted that morning for me to pick the kids up, and I agreed. I went to the house around four in the afternoon with my sister and rang the bell. Then I called his mom. She had the kids, so she met me with them at his house, and then that's when she found him lying on the floor."

"You guys were going through a divorce?" he asked.

"We were separated, and I was in the process of filing for divorce," Shante explained.

"Do you know who could have done this? It had the signs of a crime of passion," said Detective Woods.

"He had a lot of different girlfriends. As far as any of them turning into enemies, I do not know," she said.

"Where were you on the day in question?" he asked.

"I was home that morning, and then I went to my mom's before picking the kids up," she said.

"The neighbors said they saw a black luxury car parked on another street and a woman wearing a hooded sweat suit running from the house to the car," said the detective.

"I drive a silver Tahoe," Shante said.

"Your friend who just left and is sitting there, watching us— he drives a black car?" he asked.

"I don't know what kind of car he drives. He's a friend of my brother. What are you getting at?" she asked.

"I am just speculating," he replied.

"Well, speculate elsewhere. I am being as helpful as I can. I have four mourning children and a brother in the hospital," Shante said. "Any other questions?"

"No, I will keep in touch," he said, walking away.

Chapter 23

Shayla

"I am so happy to hear that, Mommy. I will be there soon. Tell Sterling I love him," said Shayla as she hung up the phone and smiled. She walked to the abandoned house where they were holding Samantha.

Before she went inside, an older lady approached her and said, "Miss, there has been a lady screaming in there all morning. I was going to call the police, but I didn't want to make the corner boys mad."

"I own this property, and a lot of addicts have been squatting in here. I am trying to get construction started as soon as possible," Shayla said.

"I saw a woman go in there one night with a jacket over her head, but I never saw her come out," said the neighbor.

"A few people have come to watch the property for me since I found some weird things in there. I haven't seen a woman, though," Shayla said.

"They were in a big white car like yours," added the woman. Shayla's heart fell. The elderly woman added, "Just watch yourself, honey. These young kids are crazy. Thanks for buying this place. You wouldn't believe the stuff that happens here." She walked away. Shayla hurried into the house to find out what was going on. She heard moaning from the room where they were keeping Samantha.

"Shut up, bitch!" Silas said. As Shayla walked into the room, she saw Samantha bent over the chair with her butt in the air.

"Are you fucking crazy?" Shayla screamed. She cried at the sight and couldn't believe her brother was so evil.

"Get the fuck out of here!" Shayla yelled at him. Silas pulled his pants up and pushed Samantha to the floor as he left. Her head hit the concrete. She was dehydrated and weak. She hadn't eaten or drunk anything in days. Shayla decided that she would end all of this. She went to the other room and pulled the prepaid phone out of her pocket, hoping it was a good time to call Hick in jail without getting him caught. He picked up on the first ring.

"Where is my wife?" he asked immediately.

"That's the only thing you care about now?"

"Yes," he said.

"She's here. I will let her go if this is it—no connect, no money, no revenge. I have a forty-five to her head right now. I will kill her if you don't agree to leave me and my family alone," she said.

"You don't have the heart," he said.

Shayla pulled the gun out of her pocketbook, cocked it, and fired a warning shot.

"Now do you believe me? I need you to let this go. I almost lost my brother, and I don't want to lose anyone else. I will let her go right now if you agree."

"All right, I will let it go," he said. Hick would tell her anything to let his wife go.

"Oh, and another thing: I am pregnant with your baby, and I am keeping it this time," she said before she hung up. She walked back to Samantha, gave her a bottle of water, and told her to drink it.

"I would never condone rape," Shayla said.

"Do you think what you did is any better?" Samantha asked, laughing.

"No, this wasn't my plan," Shayla said.

"This was your fight. You're to blame. Are you letting me go, or what?"

"You can't go to the police," Shayla said.

"I have never been a snitch. I believe people live and die by the game. I have been in it all my life. You have a lot to learn," Samantha said.

Shayla grabbed the gun and pointed it at Samantha as she walked her to the back door. It was already getting dark. Samantha walked away and then ran down the street. Shayla grabbed a trash bag and cleaned up any evidence that she and her sisters had been there. She heard someone walk into the house, and she pulled out her gun, fearing it was Samantha coming back.

"Shay!" Shanice yelled, walking in with a flashlight. She asked, "Who's watching this bitch while we go handle business?"

"I let her go," Shayla said.

"You did what?" Shanice demanded.

"I came in here and saw my freak-ass brother raping her," Shayla said.

"Fuck that! Now she knows where she was. I am sure she looked for street signs as she left," Shanice said.

"I called Hick, and he said if I let her go, that would be it," Shayla said.

"Are you fucking stupid? He told you that so you would do what he wants you to. What if she goes to the cops?" Shanice said.

"She said she wouldn't," Shayla said.

"So you just believe what anybody says now? She can get at us any way she wants now. Do you really think Hick won't come after us? Hello, stupid! There's not enough coke on the streets for everyone, and you have a connect to the best and the most of it right now. When he comes home, he's going to come after us," Shanice said angrily.

"He won't kill me. I am having his baby," Shayla said.

"I've heard it all now. What about the rest of us, the ones fighting your fucking battle while you feel sorry for the bitch even though your brother nearly died?" Shanice yelled and turned over a table.

Shayla was afraid of her sister now.

"I don't know anymore. Were you ever going to let her go?" Shayla asked.

"No! Fuck no! I was going to beat her in the head with a gun for a few hours, blow her fucking kneecaps off, and then toss her in the hospital, just like they did to Sterling!" Shanice said as tears rolled down her face.

"I am sorry, Sis. I had to end it," Shayla said, hugging her.

Shanice pulled away from her, laughed, and walked to the door. "Don't you realize—you just started it."

"Are you still going to make this run with me?" Shayla asked.

"Yes, just come on before I change my mind," Shanice said.

They didn't talk much in the car on the way to the connect. Shayla went in to pick up the product and was back out in minutes. She called Kyree when she got back in the car to let him know she was on the way.

"Where's the kitchen?" Shanice asked.

"My three-story place on Twenty-Fifth and Cecil B. Moore," Shayla said with pride. Shanice secretly texted Trez to let him know where to meet them and to look for a white Range Rover.

* * *

Kyree

"Okay, shorty, see you in a few," said Kyree, hanging up. He took a long pull of his blunt.

"She on her way?" asked Slim, Kyree's cousin. "You gonna rob and shoot shorty?" he asked.

"Yup," Kyree said as he polished his gun.

"Why, when you could just rob her, and she would never know," Slim asked.

"You would never understand," he said, looking at a bloody picture of Big Sterling, Shanice, Shayla, and Shante.

"She's bringing you this shit by herself, and she trusts you. You can just take the drugs and run."

"Shut up and just chill," Kyree said. He blasted his radio, sat on the couch, and played a video game.

Chapter 24

The End of the Beginning

Shakira

"Hello," Shakira said into the phone, just waking up from a nap. It was about six in the evening.

"You little bitch, after everything I did for you and that baby. You laughed in my face, knowing you got my son killed," Ms. Angie yelled.

"What the fuck are you talking about?" Shakira asked.

"Your brother's baby mom told a few people. The night he went missing, you had his car. Where the fuck is my son?" screamed Ms. Angie.

"I don't know what you're talking about. I am about to pay Mika a visit," Shakira yelled before she hung up. Her plans of making Silas kill Mika would make Shakira look even guiltier if the woman wound up missing. So she would beat Mika's ass for the whole neighborhood to see. Shakira threw a pair of boots on, put her hair in a ponytail, and went to Mika's house with her metal bat in her hand. She swung the bat and busted out the back windshield of Mika's truck. Then Shakira ran up the steps to Mika's front porch and busted out her front window, shattering the glass. Mika came to the door and tried to attack her. Shakira hit her in the face with the bat and then dropped the bat as Mika fell into the house. After this, Shakira ran inside and shut the door, and then Silas came downstairs.

"This bitch going around lying on me," Shakira screamed, standing over Mika and punching her face over and over as blood poured from her nose. Silas pushed Shakira off of Mika and hit his sister in the face.

"Stop! What the fuck you doing?" he said.

"You just fucking hit me! You're taking her side after all the shit we've been through?" Shakira asked. She stood up and wiped the blood off of her mouth.

"Get the fuck out of here," Silas said.

"Remember, if I go down, so will you, Silas," she said, walking outside. There were cops all over, and Steven's mom got out the cop car.

"I want her investigated for the disappearance of my son," Ms. Angie said, pointing at Shakira.

"I didn't do anything. Mika is lying about me," she said as officers approached her. Mika came to the door with her bloody face.

"I want her locked the fuck up! Look what she did to my face!" Mika screamed. She ran to attack Shakira, and they fought on the porch. Silas broke them up, pushing Shakira down the steps and onto the ground.

"Ma'am, please put your hands behind your back," said an officer as he read Shakira her rights and handcuffed her wrists. As she got in the cop car she saw a guy holding her metal bat walking away quickly. She noticed that she had never cleaned Steven's blood off the bat after killing him. As long as the bat was not in her house, they had no evidence on her. It was the only thing that linked her to his murder. It was Silas and Mika's word against hers.

*   *   *

Shayla and Shanice

"Shit, I hate when people park in front of my building. I like to get in and get out," Shayla said. Shanice pretended to play a game on her phone as she texted Trez to let him know they were pulling up. He texted back that he saw them.

"Are you coming up with me? I wanted to show you the apartments," asked Shayla.

"No, I will wait here. Just call me if you have a problem," said Shanice.

"That won't happen with Kyree. I think he has a little crush on me," Shayla said, getting out of the car. She grabbed the duffel bags and carried them to the house. She pressed the intercom button for the apartment on the top floor.

"Yo!" Kyree said.

"It's me!" she said. He buzzed the door open and she walked in. Immediately, she felt cold metal being pressed against the back of her head.

"Don't make a sound. Keep moving," Trez said through a ski mask. He looked at Shayla's profile and couldn't believe that Shanice had set him up to rob her sister. He walked her through the hallway.

"Why can't we just take the drugs and leave," Jermaine said, holding the gun.

"You're right," Trez said. He knocked Shayla to the floor, snatched the bags, and hit her in the head with the gun. Shanice saw Trez run off and jump in his car. She jumped out of Shayla's car, putting a bullet in the chamber of her .45.

In the apartment, Kyree said, "Go downstairs and help her with the bags. That's probably what's taking so long."

"You want me to help her before you rob and kill her?" Slim said, laughing. He didn't see her on the second story, so he walked to the first floor and saw Shayla on the floor with blood all over. Just then, Shanice used Shayla's keys and walked into the building. She found Slim standing over Shayla with a gun. Shanice and Slim quickly pointed their guns at each other. Slim called for Kyree, and as his hands began to shake, he let a shot go. It missed Shanice, but she returned fire and hit him in the middle of the head. He fell to the hallway floor. Kyree was upstairs, listening to loud music and unable to distinguish the gunshots. Shanice dragged her sister out of the house, and two men who walking down the street helped her put Shayla in the car. Shayla was still breathing but losing a lot of blood. Shanice knew she had to get away from the apartment and take her sister to the hospital.

"You did not see me," Shanice said, giving each man $200 and speeding off. Kyree heard the car tires screech and realized that something was wrong. He ran downstairs and found his little cousin in a pool of blood. Shayla was gone, and there were no drugs.

"Oh my God!" he screamed.

*   *   *

Shante

Shante had seen Little Sterling earlier that day, and she was in good spirits. She called Jared, but he wouldn't answer. He texted her, saying that his sister came home and had been through a lot. He would call in the morning. Shante texted him back, telling him she would pray for him. Shante had all the kids and was unable to find any of her sisters. Her phone rang with a call from someone at the police station.

"Hello," she said.

"Sis, I am in trouble. I got locked up. I have money at my house. Can you go get it tonight? I will call you when I get my bail," Shakira said as quickly as she could.

"Okay. Where is it in the house?" Shante asked.

"In the safe in my bedroom closet. The combination is daddy's birthday."

"Okay, I got it," she said, hanging up. Shante called Shayla's phone, but she got no answer, so she called Shanice's phone.

"Hello!" Shanice said in a panic.

"Where the fuck are you and Shayla? 'Kira is in jail. I have to get her bail money," Shante said as tears fell from her eyes.

"Oh my god, what happened?" Shanice asked.

"I don't know," Shante said.

Shanice said, "Shayla was robbed at one of her apartment buildings. She was hit in the head, and she's not doing so well."

"Why is all of this happening to our family?" Shante asked, crying harder.

"Maybe Shay will have the answer when she wakes up," Shanice said with hate in her voice.

"Let me call Silas. Where are you guys?" Shante asked.

"Temple, where else?" Shanice said.

"Okay, I will be there soon," Shante said. She looked at all the kids, who were asleep on the floor. She called her aunt Nancy, who lived nearby.

"Hello," said her aunt sleepily when she answered the phone.

"Aunt Nancy, I need you more than ever. Shakira is in jail, and Shayla is in the hospital—someone robbed her, and she is not doing well. And Mom is already at the hospital with Little Sterling," she said in one breath.

"Okay, stop it. Bring all the kids here, and I will take care of them."

Shante woke them up and piled them all in her truck. She was at her aunt's house in no time.

"Thanks, Aunt Nancy," she said.

"No problem, baby. Call me as soon as you can," her aunt said. Shante called Silas as soon as she got back in the car.

"Hello," he said.

"Oh my God, Silas, Shakira is in jail, and Shayla is in the hospital because someone beat her with a gun," Shante said.

"You know what? That's what she gets after all the shit we're going through because of her. Fuck 'Kira. She came over here, beat Mika up, and broke our windows. I don't want to be bothered with y'all bitches," he yelled into the phone.

"What do you mean? We are supposed to be a family. I'm sure Shakira whooped Mika's ass for a reason," Shante said, defending her sister.

"Fuck out of here with that family shit. Fuck family—this is my family!" he said, hanging up on her. Shante was beyond hurt. She had to hold her family together and did not know what to do. When she got to the hospital, Shayla was still unconscious in ER trauma care. Shanice was sitting in the waiting room, sleeping.

"Sis, what's up?" Shante asked as she sat down next to her.

"I am waiting for the doctor to give me news," Shanice said.

"Did you call Mommy?" Shante asked.

"No, and don't call her until we know what's up. She has been through so much already," Shanice said.

"I know. I am going to go upstairs and check on her. Call me as soon as you hear something," Shante said.

While Shanice sat there, she called Trez, whom she was supposed to hear from.

"Yeah?" he said.

"What the fuck you mean?" Shanice said.

"What you made me do was fucked up," Trez said.

"You let me worry about that," Shanice said.

"There were six kilos," Trez said.

"I want my half in cash, and don't try any funny shit. You've got five days," she said before she hung up.

When Shante jumped on the elevator to see her mom, she ran right into Jared.

"Oh my God, what are you doing here?" she asked.

"My sister is here. Someone found her passed out on the street. It was a good thing she was still wearing a medical ID bracelet from the fainting spells she had when she was pregnant. The hospital called my family as soon as she got here. Someone beat her with a gun, starved her, and raped her. I am so sick right now—I could kill the person who did this to her," Jared said.

"No, it's not worth it. I feel so bad for her. I am here to see my mom and make sure she is okay," Shante said.

They rode the elevator together and got off on the same floor. Jared stopped at room 515, where his sister was. Shante glanced into the room. There were so many people there that she didn't see the woman's face clearly, but it looked very bad. Shante kissed Jared on the lips and approached her brother's room, 535.

Ms. Sandy was asleep in the recliner, and Sterling was awake, watching ESPN.

"Hi, Bro," she said calmly.

"Hi," he said.

"You watching sports?" she asked. He nodded as tears rolled down his face. She cried too, because they both knew he would never play ball again. She noticed his heart rate and blood pressure were extremely high. His face was pale, and he was sweating all over. Shante called a nurse to check on him. The machines beep as doctors ran into the room.

"What happened?" Ms. Sandy said, beginning to cry. The doctors asked them both to leave. Ms. Sandy and Shante ran out of the room, scared to look at Sterling, but the door was still open. Shante called Shanice and told her to come upstairs. The doctors started CPR on Little Sterling. Shante and Ms. Sandy stood in the hall and cried, hoping he would live through this. Shanice arrived just as Sterling flatlined.

"No! Why!" Shanice cried and fell to the floor, and some nurses came to help her.

Little Sterling died from a blood infection on January 7, 2013, at 1:30 a.m. Shante handled the paperwork so that the funeral home would pick up his body from the hospital.

"Where are Shayla, Shakira, and Silas?" Ms. Sandy asked as the three women walked to the car.

"Shakira got locked up earlier, and Shayla was robbed at gunpoint and pistol-whipped," Shante said quickly.

"What!" Ms. Sandy yelled. Shanice hung her head.

"Shayla is in stable condition. She just has a concussion," Shanice said.

"This is your fault. You just had to play the vigilante, didn't you? I heard about the kidnapping shit," Ms. Sandy said to Shanice.

"How is it my fault?" Shanice asked.

"You are always in the middle of something. All this started when they ran up in your house," Ms. Sandy said in tears.

"I can take care of my own shit, for your information. This all started when Shayla decided to rob her boyfriend for his drugs and money. Did she tell you that? I tried to help get my brother back alive!" Shanice announced.

"You tortured her for a week. You killed Sterling," Ms. Sandy said.

"She told you that? I did it all by myself. I had to clean up this bitch's mess, and I got blamed for everything. You know what? Fuck all of this. You always choose her over me. I am through trying to work shit out. My little brother is gone now. That fucking bitch Mika got my sister locked up. Y'all are against me. After the funeral, you won't have to worry about me. I hope that bitch suffers for letting this shit happen." Shanice walked away.

*　*　*

Hick

Before long, a relative of Samantha's visited Hick.

"Why are you here?" Hick asked.

"I told you I want to help. I am not a kid. Who did this?" he asked.

Hick told him the story of his relationship with Shayla.

Hick said, "She couldn't have done this alone. It had to be the brother and Shanice. Shanice is in the streets like that— Shakira too. Shante just goes with the flow. And they all stick together."

"I will send you a picture of the whole family with addresses. If the youngest is still breathing, take him out too. I will tell you exactly what to do," Hick said.

"Say no more. They ride together, they die together," said the visitor, getting up to leave. Diamond sat in the visiting room, reading lips the whole time.

*   *   *

Diamond

A week later, Shayla's phone rang, and Shante picked it up.

"Shayla!" yelled the caller.

"No, Shayla is not accepting calls. She just got out of the hospital, and we are burying my brother today," Shante said.

"This is Diamond. What happened?" she asked.

"She was robbed last week, and our brother died the same day," Shante explained.

"I heard about Sterling. I am so sorry, but this is urgent," Diamond said.

Shayla agreed to take the call.

"I have been trying to call you all week. A guy came to the prison to visit Hick, and Hick told the guy he would send him a picture of you, your sisters, and your mother, with your addresses. I stopped the letter. It was addressed to JD, who's supposed to be his brother. Hick is going to be released from prison this morning," Diamond said in one breath.

"He is? But how?" Shayla asked. She instantly felt pain in her stomach.

"What's wrong?" Shante asked Shayla.

"Nothing," she said.

"I will call you later," Diamond said as she watched Jermaine throw a bag of money on her bed.

"What is this?" Diamond asked.

"Don't worry. Why don't you go shopping?" Jermaine said, tossing her a Gucci bag with cash in it.

Chapter 25

The Funeral

It was a rainy day. The whole family stood around Sterling's casket at the cemetery and cried. There had been a large funeral at the recreation center where he spent most his time. No one spoke a word to each other now. As they all got back into the limo, Shayla had a panic attack. She was upset and scared out of her mind, not knowing what Hick was going to do. Shante consoled her, but Shanice, Shakira, and Silas paid her no mind. When the limo pulled up to Ms. Sandy's house, Shanice and Shakira went to Shakira's car and piled all their kids inside.

"So you are all just going to leave instead of supporting each other," Ms. Sandy said from the porch.

Everyone just looked back at her silently.

"I am going into the house. My heart is broken too. Please stay for me if not for each other. I love all of you, despite what some of you might think," Ms. Sandy pleaded.

Just as she turned to go in the house, they heard a bunch of motorcycles nearby. Shanice noticed the first one as it turned the corner. A man wearing a ski mask sat in front of a woman carrying a machine gun. They were followed by three other bikes holding people with machine guns.

"Get down now!" Shanice screamed. Shots were fired as everyone screamed and tried to find cover. The attackers shot up Ms. Sandy's house in minutes. After the motorcycles finally left, there were shell casings everywhere.

"Oh my God!" Shante screamed. She called 911.

"I need an ambulance—hurry please! There's blood everywhere," Shante yelled into her phone.

"Oh my God, somebody help us!" Shante shouted. She threw her body across Ms. Sandy, and her daughter who lay in blood on the porch.

Read *Savage Sisters: Part Two*, coming soon.